Petrichor

Melanie Rees

I0603089

PETRICHOR

Copyright 2021
Hague Publishing
PO Box 451
Bassendean, Western AUSTRALIA 6934
Email: contact@haguepublishing.com
Web: www.haguepublishing.com

Paperback ISBN: 978-0-6488346-2-5
EBook ISBN: 978-0-6488346-1-8

Cover: Petrichor by Jade Zivanovic of Steam Power Studios
(https://www.steampowerstudios.com.au/)

Typeset Garamond 12/13

We respectfully acknowledge the Traditional Custodians of Australia as our first storytellers and creators of culture in this land, and acknowledge their continuing connection to Country. In the spirit of Reconciliation, we pay our respect to them, their cultures, and to elders both past, present, and emerging.

15% of the publisher's revenue from the sale of this book will be donated to the following charities:

Rural Aid (https://www.ruralaid.org.au)
and
Beyond Blue (https://www.beyondblue.org.au)

CHAPTER 1

Even from inside the ute, Clayton could see the blood trickling down the lamb's neck. His dad pulled up alongside the injured animal. As the grunting of the engine stuttered to a halt, the sheep's relentless bleating took over, echoing across Paddle Creek Station.

"You staying in the car?" Dad asked.

Clayton tore his eyes from the lamb and looked up at his dad, the rifle already firmly in his grasp. "No. I can help." He popped on his khaki bucket hat and followed his dad out onto the dusty paddock with Rusty eagerly yapping at his heels.

"Get that mutt away from here!" Dad yelled, as he loaded the rifle.

Mutt? Clayton rubbed the kelpie behind the ears. She was no mutt. She'd been Davo's dog, but she was still part of the family. "Why can't she come? She's not scared, are you girl?" Clayton scratched under her collar and Rusty's hind leg started twitching in gleeful circles in sync with his scratching.

"She's in the way." His dad glared at him.

Clayton grabbed Rusty's collar and directed her back towards the ute. She walked in circles a few times and plonked herself down in a tiny strip of shade beside the vehicle.

Clayton sat with her. He didn't want to watch his dad shoot the lamb, but something compelled him to do so. A bloody chunk had been torn from the lamb's neck and a ripe stench wafted from the wound. The lamb's body quivered and flies buzzed above it ready to descend.

"Can you help it?" asked Clayton, although he knew the loaded rifle already answered his question.

Dad cocked the rifle. "You don't have to watch."

"I'm okay. I saw Dav . . ." Clayton noticed his dad's forehead pucker into little wrinkles. "I've seen it done before."

"Hmmm," Dad mumbled.

"He hit a roo once when we were doing doughnuts in the paddock. He had to shoot –"

"Clay! I don't care what *he* did. And if you mention him again I swear to the bleeding rain gods I'll lose my shit." He pushed his Akubra back from his eyes and placed the rifle to the lamb's temple.

Rusty barked, perhaps in defence of Davo's memory.

Clayton pressed his forehead against Rusty's snout. "It's okay, girl," he whispered, trying to reassure himself as much as her.

The gun blast assaulted his ears and sent a shudder through his body.

His dad looked up. Clayton expected to see grief, but his face was deadpan underneath the Akubra.

"I'll bury it and then we'll fix that fence." Dad's anger had subsided.

Clayton picked up the shovel lying in the back of the ute. "How deep do I dig?"

His dad held out his hand.

"I can do it," Clayton said, beginning to dig. As he did the shovel ricocheted against the hard ground, jarring his elbows. In the hot air, Clayton's t-shirt stuck to his back even though he'd only managed a few centimetres. Keeping the spade vertical, he plunged it into the ground again and stomped on either side of the shovelhead. His small frame did little to bury it.

"Give it here." His dad snatched the shovel before Clayton could object. "Too much time with your head in those books and not enough time with your feet on the ground doing real work."

Davo had always been the musclier one, just like their dad. Even ignoring the age gap between them, Clayton's older brother had been the real farmer in his dad's eyes. Tucked away behind the kitchen door, Davo's blue line on the giraffe height chart had always been an inch higher than Clayton's red line at the same age. Now the giraffe was gone, torn down along with all the other reminders of Davo. Thinking about Davo's death stung, but as hard as he tried, Clayton couldn't recall the days leading up to his funeral.

Dad handed the shovel to Clayton, grabbed the lamb's hind legs and slid it into the shallow grave, leaving a thin trail of blood barely distinguishable from the red earth underneath.

He'd seen kangaroos shot, sheep dying, and Davo's casket, but there was something brutal and final in his dad's actions and expression that reverberated in Clayton's chest.

Clayton shovelled the loose dirt over the carcass, although most of it billowed into the air as if the dust had a mind of its own. Wisps spiralled into the air like tendrils. As if searching, the dust drifted towards him. It looked so solid, as if he could grab it. Clayton reached out a hand.

"Clay! Come on."

He turned. His dad sat inside the ute, tapping the steering wheel. Rusty was already perched on the tray top.

Clayton climbed in, hoisting his feet up to avoid the farming debris that littered the passenger side floor. "Can Rusty sit with us? She was allowed up here before –"

"Fu . . . Bugg . . . Darn! Lift your legs." Dad bit his lip.

Clayton looked down. His feet rested on the rifle.

Dad double checked the safety and placed the rifle on the bench seat between them.

"Keep your feet to one side of the other tools. There's no room for Rusty."

And yet there was room for all this junk. Clayton knew there was no point arguing though. With his legs perched on an angle on top of the tools, he stared out the window as the car took off.

They drove along an old internal fence line, not that there was much of a fence left. Drifting sands obscured all but the top strand of rusted barbwire. In some sections, there was no wire at all, but the star droppers still stood defiant: a last testimonial to all that once was. A few klicks ahead, the hills of the conservation reserve loomed. Between the farm and the reserve, Davo's property was covered with saltbush untouched for months.

Clayton turned to his dad. "Why won't you tell me how he died?"

"Huh?" His dad faced him, wide-eyed, perhaps shocked at the abruptness of the question.

"It's just, I don't remember." Clayton struggled to recall his last intact memory of his brother. He remembered them fishing way back when Paddle Creek had water trickling down from the reserve, and an image of Davo and him cleaning out fertiliser from the seeder bins. But the past few months were as hazy as the horizon.

"Dad?" he prompted.

His dad turned from Clayton, focusing on the road. "We're not talking 'bout it."

"Why won't you or Mum tell —"

"Shut it, Clay!" Dad's ancient hands grasped the steering wheel tightly.

Clayton bit his tongue, trying to hold back tears. He wound down the window, using it as an excuse to turn away and conceal his face, but as his dad drove over the cattle grid onto the next paddock the shuddering of the ute dislodged a tear and it rolled down his check and onto his lap.

The wind picked up and tossed whiffs of dust into the air. Clayton let the hot air dry his eyes. The breeze swept through the window, stirring the flies that had been content to cling to the inside of the windscreen. Clayton swatted at the little black beasts, but his dad seemed content to let them dance around his eyes and cracked lips. It was as if they were clinging to a carcass. Clayton wanted to swipe them away. There was still life in Dad, somewhere – deep down.

Dad leaned over the steering wheel and stared out the windscreen.

Clayton followed his gaze. Grey storm clouds brewed over the hills. He exchanged a quick glance with his dad and saw the faintest hint of a smile.

"Ain't that a beautiful sight." Clayton heard the change in his dad's voice from its usual monotonous tone to something that almost resembled optimism. Dad didn't elaborate further, but some things didn't need words.

Not far ahead, the northern boundary fence ran for kilometres in both directions – dead straight – dissecting Davo's and his parent's properties like a scalpel. His brother's old bluestone house stood prominently just beyond the fence. Davo's paddocks still maintained a trace of fresh growth like an untrimmed beard. Tiny seedlings poked through the dry plains, fighting the earth's brittle crust. In comparison, their property, with its crisp chewed saltbush, looked like it had a bristly five o'clock shadow.

His dad stopped at the gate and sat, eyes fixed on Davo's house. Clutching the steering wheel, his knuckles bulged, gangly, and arthritic. They turned whiter with each passing moment. Outside the skies grumbled, snapping him out of his daze.

"We might just be able to wring some rains out of these clouds." His dad's lips turned upwards, but his eyes didn't flinch and his smile lines didn't crease. "This could finally be the break we need."

Clayton jumped from the passenger seat. Dust had painted the sides of the ute red and he scribbled "wash me" on the door with his finger.

"Nudge reckons as soon as you wash your car it will rain. Says it's better than a rain dance." Clayton danced up towards his father with one arm in the air, stamping his feet.

Clayton looked up at him expectantly, waiting for a smile.

"Aren't you're meant to be a teenager now?" Dad's gaze remained fixed on Davo's property.

At least the corellas sitting on the rim of a water trough found it amusing and gave a chorus of squawks.

"How we going to fix this mess?" Dad tugged at the fence.

The Ringlock fence had come adrift from the wooden posts and the top strand of barbwire sagged along the ground. But in one section, the fence was still taut, and there, pinned to the barbwire by their tails, a dozen fox carcasses were lined up. The oldest kill was barely recognisable. Fur had disintegrated and the skeleton was starting to protrude through the leathery skin. The wind ruffled the fur of the last fox. A brown coat still covered its body except for the mange at the base of its tail.

"Why haven't they all decomposed?" Clayton asked.

"Hmm?" Dad looked up from the fence.

"The foxes, how long have they been here? How long does it take to rot?"

"Dunno. I ain't been up to the boundary fence since . . ." The furrow in Dad's brow deepened and his complexion darkened, as if the approaching storm clouds had briefly swept across his face. "I don't know, Clay. Do something useful and get me the fencing strainer, staples, and hammer from the ute."

Clayton stood motionless. "Which one's the strainer?"

"It's got the chain attached. Get with the program."

Clayton strolled to the ute. The front was a mess: tools, bolts and empty slugs were lumped together, tangled among offcuts of fencing wire and pink baling twine. Clayton carefully moved the rifle out of the way, grasping it by the barrel.

"Whoa! Don't touch that!" His dad snatched the rifle from Clayton.

"Sorry. It was in the way and I couldn't find the tool."

"*Never* handle that yourself." Dad pointed at a metal contraption that looked like someone had welded a couple of clamps, a metal bar, and chain together. It was more like some evil clawed bear trap than a tool.

Dad grabbed it and the other bits and pieces he needed and returned to the fence. "You gotta watch this. You'll need to learn to mend fences someday."

Dad connected two loose ends of wire with the chain, levered the bar 'til it was tight and did something with the ends of the wire. His dad's left index and middle finger were missing their fingertips from a farming accident long before Clayton was born, but despite his arthritis and missing fingertips his calloused hands were more dexterous than they looked.

Clayton scratched his head. "I'm not built for this."

"Course you are. It's in your blood. The Hopper gene . . . is tough." His dad's voice cracked.

Wind stirred. Dad coughed on a mouthful of dust, said some words Clayton's mum would never have approved of, and resumed mending the fence.

The darkening clouds crept over the ridge of hills and covered them in shadow as his dad worked. The shadows inched their way towards Davo's homestead. It used to be the shearers' quarters, but to Clayton it would always be his brother's house. He unlatched the gate, where tiny white snails smothered the rotting wooden post. It squealed as he pushed it ajar. Half a year had gone by since he'd been here, but the homestead looked the same as it had always done.

A gust of wind spun the rusted windmill, making it creak, and saltbush bowed with the force as if praying to the house.

Amid Davo's saltbush country and homestead, there was familiarity. Memory tugged at Clayton's subconscious. Images of them riding on the quad bike and sitting on the front porch admiring a winter crop as Rusty chased galahs. He remembered when Davo moved out. His brother had been so excited.

"Dad's carved me off a bit of his land to help get me going," Davo had boasted.

"You're miles away. I'll never see you."

"Sure you will. When Dad's too old and cranky to hop on a tractor you'll have Dad's place and we can manage both properties together as one."

"He'll still be on the tractor when he's a hundred."

Davo had laughed with his usual hearty chuckle. "So take the quad bike. You can come round whenever you want," he said, pointing to Dad's chunky green beast.

"But I can't open the cocky gate between your and Dad's property."

"Come on, buddy. Even Mum can open and close that one. I'll replace it for you. Got an old swing gate in the shed. Much easier to open with these little muscles." Davo had squeezed Clayton's biceps like they were jelly and laughed. "Look." He disappeared inside and returned cradling a tiny ball of fur so red it could've blended into the soil at sunset. "I'm going to make Dad so proud. Got me own sheep dog and everything." They'd both loved that puppy from the moment it started frolicking in the paddock: all lanky legs, floppy ears and smiles.

"Clayton!" His dad's voice rumbled like a road train, bringing Clayton out of his reverie. "Get back here now!"

His dad stood by the open gate, unable to place a foot on Davo's land.

"Why?" asked Clayton. He stood his ground, but his voice lost its resolve.

"Coz I said so."

When his dad uttered those words, he knew it was the end of the discussion. He dawdled to the gate, glancing back to Davo's house.

"Hurry up!"

"Hold your horses, Dad. I'm coming."

"I ain't got no horses. I've just got a flock of sheep that might start roaming too far if we don't fix this bleeding fence. And I got a son who's never going to be a farmer if he doesn't come back from la-la land."

Wind stirred, enveloping the old homestead in a cloud of red dust. Dry and bitter at the back of Clayton's throat, it made him cough. He hurried back onto their property.

His dad yanked the gate. "Close, you mongrel." He kicked the post, jolting it far enough for the latch to reach. He turned to Clayton. "Don't go near that house. You hear me?" Dad's eyes were as wide and wild as the approaching storm.

Clayton nodded, unable to speak, his vocal chords losing more than their resolve.

Rank tumbleweed rolled across the paddock like runaway Ferris wheels until the fence caught the plants in its grip. Clouds streamed across the sky and merged like hands intertwining, fingers clasped tight. They rumbled in a passionate embrace. A raindrop fell on the back of Clayton's neck, cooling him under his t-shirt. Another fell on his cheek, and then the storm clouds rushed southward without another drop – the honeymoon over as quickly as it began.

"Ha!" His dad laughed at the sky.

The tail winds of the storm stripped more soil from the earth. Clayton shielded his eyes and suddenly a shot echoed across the plains. Corellas on the water trough squawked and took flight.

"Is that all you got?" Dad aimed his rifle at the receding storm clouds. "Is that all you bloody well got! Come back here." His tone of voice was foreign to Clayton and he retreated to the ute.

"Hah, I'll give you some lead, then you might be heavy enough to drop rain." Dad cocked the gun and took another shot at the sky.

"We're tough." He strode up and down the fence line, his joints forgetting their arthritis. "We're bleedin' tough, you hear me. We can cope with the dry."

"Dad?" Clayton couldn't hear his own voice, but he didn't know whether it was because the rifle was making so much noise or because he hadn't actually spoken. He shook as another shot rang out. Rusty growled at Dad as if he were a stranger.

"Dad, stop!" Clayton squatted, clasped his ears with his hands and put his head to his knees. "Stop it, stop it, stop it."

"You! Are you bloody well looking at me?"

Clayton dared to glance up. A bullet collided with a dead fox on the fence. The rifle fired again, hitting the fox in its side. The carcass jolted with the force and its head lifted backwards. Although its eyes were sunken and closed, the fox appeared to look in Clayton's direction.

He turned his gaze from the fox, crawled along the dusty earth towards Rusty and wrapped his arms around the kelpie's neck. "Dad! Please."

His dad fired again and again until the fox's torso split open. Dad shut his eyes tight, screwed up his face and fired one more shot. With the impact of the last bullet, the fox launched itself from the fence and landed on Davo's side in a heap, its legs splayed out at odd tangents, its amber eyes opened and stared directly at Clayton. Its lips parted and the dead fox grinned.

CHAPTER 2

Stones popped like firecrackers against the mudguard and chassis as Dad detoured across the middle of the paddock. He was taking the shortest route possible. Fleeing. He hadn't even cared that Clayton had insisted on going on the tray- top with Rusty. She nuzzled Clayton as if she could sense his concern.

He stood, holding the roll bar, and gazed behind the vehicle. Dust billowed up from the wheels and soon red haze obscured everything behind them. As the vehicle slowed, the dust cloud drew closer. A plume extended towards them like an arm, reaching out for its prey.

The ute came to a standstill. Rusty growled. And a faint voice whispered upon the breeze, as if lost in the haze.

"Oi! You deaf?" Dad shouted from the garden. "We're home."

Clayton looked back at the paddock. The dust appeared to run away from the vehicle, but that was ludicrous. Dust couldn't run. Clayton hopped off the ute and walked a few metres towards the moving dust. The hazy mass slunk into the earth, but a whiff of dust re-emerged and seemed to turn in his direction. Clayton shut his eyes and shook his head. When he reopened them, all the dust had vanished, revealing a slab of blue sky sitting atop a slab of ochre.

Hunched over her laptop on the kitchen table, his mum glanced up as they entered. Clayton noticed Mum's eyes probing. Somehow, she knew something wasn't right and yet all she said was, "Walter?" There seemed to be a question tagged onto his name like a hook on a fishing line trying to lure him in.

Dad didn't bite though, and she didn't cast any more questions.

"We didn't finish fixing the fence," Clayton said, trying to fill the silence and sway his dad to talk about what happened.

His mum looked at them in turn. She seemed to be searching for answers but was unable to ask the question.

"We ran out of time, Emily. We found a lamb injured on our way so we had to take care of that." His dad's explanation was lame. They had plenty of time.

"We could've finished but . . ." Clayton looked to his mum to fill in the blanks.

"That's alright," his mother said with forced cheerfulness. "We'll get Nudge to fix it tomorrow. He's been looking for more farmhand work. If we pay him mate's rates we might be able to afford a day's pay." She peered at her laptop screen and the cheerfulness evaporated from her voice. "It'll be okay."

No, it wouldn't. Dad wasn't okay. There was no sadness, no anger, no worry. Couldn't she see the emptiness in his eyes? But she didn't press the issue, didn't quibble or bat an eyelid; instead, she closed the laptop and checked the oven.

"Are you hungry, Clay, sweetie?" she asked. "I've made fish mornay and that salad you like with the crispy noodles."

Clayton waited for his dad to chip in with a joke about his food preferences, but there was nothing.

"It's a nice mornay. Reggie gave us some fish when he delivered the hay bales this afternoon."

Clayton reflected on their days sitting on the riverbank at the mention of fish: three rods buried in the sandy banks; an Esky with juice for him, ginger beer for Davo, and a proper beer for Dad. And constant chatter.

"Maybe we could go fishing too, before the school holidays end." Clayton sat down next to his dad.

"How many bales did Reggie drop off?" Dad asked, ignoring him.

His mum hesitated. "He only had half a load left."

"What?" Dad smacked his palms on the table and stood up.

"But he was kind enough to give us some silage," she added hurriedly, "to help tide us over for a few weeks as well."

"Dad? Please. Can we go fishing? Like we used to. Remember when we used to go with Da –"

"Clay, sweetie." Although his mum's voice was as sweet as honey, it stung like a bee. "We don't need to talk about this now." She put three plates on the table. Sweet smelling steam rose from them, but neither of his parents were paying any attention to the food.

"She'll be right once it rains." It sounded as if Dad were speaking in a vacuum, the air having sucked all passion from his voice.

Clayton stared at the towering pile of mornay and salad. He prodded at the food with his fork while thinking how to construct his words. But he wasn't even sure what he was trying say.

Rusty licked Clayton's shins and looked up expectantly. He placed a piece of fish on the floor for her, trying not to attract his parents' attention.

"I was thinking we could get a loan for some more feed." His mum hadn't sat down to eat yet and his dad hadn't touched his food. Clayton rubbed Rusty behind the ears, hoping she'd be patient enough to wait for their leftovers.

"Another loan?" Dad grunted.

"There's a small bit of feed up north," Clayton said.

"No, there's not," Dad said.

Mum wrung her hands on the tea towel.

"Yeah, there is. Remember he planted that saltbush feedlot. I saw it today."

"The northern property isn't ours to graze," Dad said. "If it rains, everything'll be okay. We just need a good soaking."

He stared out the kitchen window. "As far as I'm concerned that whole property doesn't exist."

Rusty rested her paws on the kitchen table, knocking Clayton's plate. It clattered against the table and Dad spun as Rusty extended her slobbery tongue towards the food.

"Get that stupid mutt out of here. Take her outside!" he yelled.

"But it's hot," Clayton said.

"I don't care. I don't want her slobbering about the kitchen when we're eating. I don't want *that* dog in here at all."

"But—"

"No buts." His dad grabbed Rusty's collar and dragged her towards the back door. Rusty pawed at the floor trying to reach the table; her tongue drooped longingly towards the food.

"Don't!" Clayton ran to Rusty's side.

"Then take her outside!" His dad released his grip and returned to the table.

Clayton squatted next to Rusty, cuddling her around her neck, partly to prevent her attacking the kitchen table, partly to calm his own nerves.

"Walt," Mum began cautiously. "Maybe. Just maybe, it's a possibility. Letting the stock into his . . . into the northern property. It's been a few months. Maybe it's time—"

"Shut it, woman!" His father hurled his plate of food at the far wall. The china shattered like confetti, tinkling onto the lino floor.

Rusty pounced on the remnant fish mornay.

"Get her out!" Dad bellowed.

Clayton looked to his mum for support, but she stood by the kitchen sink twisting the tea towel between her hands so much her fingers turned bright red.

"I gotta do work," his dad mumbled, storming out of the kitchen.

"Clay, sweetie, Rusty doesn't need to be inside." She tried to say it calmly, but there was no denying the quiver in her voice. She turned her back on him. "Rusty could do with some fresh air."

With a trembling hand, Clayton picked up a chunk of fish from the floor. There was no need to ask Rusty to follow. She licked Clayton's hand all the way to the front porch.

He sat on the top step and opened his palm. Rusty's salivating tongue searched out every centimetre of Clayton's hand. The warm twilight air stirred, drying the dog's slobber in seconds. Any trace of clouds and the possibility of rain had drifted away. Wind wafted a plume of dust into the air like a finger beckoning him to follow.

Clayton rubbed Rusty's ears. "Come on, girl. We'll make Dad happy again. We can finish fixing the fence for him." He walked across the back paddock to their massive, galvanised shed, Rusty trailed close on his heels.

Hay bales from Reggie and sacks of grain filled the middle of the shed. His father's tractor, header, quad bike, and a mishmash of tools cluttered one end. Beyond it Davo's old tractor sat alone in the far corner – forlorn and forgotten.

Clayton made his way through the minefield of equipment and plucked the spare key to the quad bike from a hook under the workbench, where Davo had always hid it so they could do doughnuts in the wheat crops at night and pretend they were UFO marks.

Clayton turned the ignition and the old beast spluttered into action. "Up, Rusty."

She leaped onto the back of the quad bike and held her head over the side, sniffing the breeze.

He drove in a daze. The quad bike shuddered as he passed over the cattle grid, but besides that he didn't notice much of the scenery. The sun sank slowly into the earth as if it were in no hurry to welcome another day.

The sky had turned pink by the time he reached the northern boundary. Silhouetted in the failing light, Davo's old homestead looked like a cardboard cut-out pasted onto the horizon.

Clayton dismounted. "Down, girl."

Rusty stood on the back of the quad, growling.

"Cut it out."

Rusty barked again.

Clayton turned. There was nothing around them except the bare paddocks shining red as the sun sank behind the hills. "What's wrong, girl? The gun's not here."

Clayton patted her and walked to the fence. Tools and empty shells remained, scattered on the ground.

He grabbed the fencing strainers. "So how do I work this thing?"

He tried to feed a wire into the strainer, but it didn't want to stay in place. The light was fast disappearing and he could barely make out what he was doing. Why didn't he think to bring a torch?

Clayton turned to Rusty. "Nailing would be easier, don't you think?"

Rusty spoke back, but it wasn't her usual cheerful bark.

"Cut it out, girl," said Clayton, squinting at the ground for the relevant tools. He patted the ground until he found the hammer and small plastic bag that held the fencing staples. He placed a U-shaped nail over the wire and tapped it lightly with the hammer until the wood grabbed it. He clutched the hammer in two hands. His dad would never approve of the girlish method but it was easier this way. He bashed it, and the nail bent at a right angle.

Padding up beside him, Rusty growled with her head low to the ground.

"It's crooked, but it's not that bad, girl." Clayton looked at his efforts and at the nails that his dad had knocked neatly into the wooden posts. "Okay, I should try again." He turned the hammer around and tried to rip the nail out, but it didn't budge. "Pliers? Dad had pliers here somewhere."

Clayton kneeled down and scanned the ground. He patted the soil beneath him, feeling in the dim light for the pliers; instead, his hand rested on something soft. He peered closer then recoiled, realising it was the tail of the dead fox poking through the fence. A fetid breeze swept across the paddock that smelled like rotten fruit: ripe and sweet, but also putrid.

Rusty nuzzled up alongside him and whimpered in his ear.

Clayton turned to the kelpie and rubbed her ears. "Yeah, I know, girl. The foxes reek." He scratched her under the collar. "You normally like sniffing and rolling in anything smelly: cow pats, dead mice –"

Rusty interrupted with a snarl and bared her teeth.

"What's got into you? There's nothing out there." Clayton peered into the darkness in the direction Rusty was looking. "It's just a dead fox . . ." Clayton's voice trailed off as a lump caught in his throat. The fox was there a second ago. He was sure it was there a second ago.

"Hello?" Clayton whispered.

Rusty growled with her head to the ground. She leaped over the fence and darted towards Davo's homestead, barking furiously.

"Rusty!" Disorientated by the darkness, Clayton stood. "Come back! We're not allowed over there."

There was no sign of her. If something dragged the fox away, it would have to be pretty big. With that thought in mind, Clayton picked up the hammer and felt his way along the fence line until he reached the gate. The outline of Davo's house was just visible in the moonlight.

It's just Davo's house. There's nothing to be scared of. There's no reason why Dad should care if I go over there.

Keeping his eyes fixed on the house, he fumbled with the stubborn latch and swung the gate open.

There's nothing to be scared of. His heart thumped so strongly in his chest it hurt his ribs. *Nothing to be scared of.*

He took a step forward. Then another. The soil's crust crunched under his shoes like crispbread. A twig snapped under his foot.

Alongside the bluestone building something rustled.

Clinging to the shadows of the old homestead a dark shape hunched over as if in pain, its snout low to the ground.

"Rusty?" Clayton dropped the hammer and ran forward, praying she wasn't injured.

Curled up in a fetal position, the figure whined.

Nearby him, something snarled. Clayton turned. Rusty was there, baring her teeth.

"You're okay!" Relieved, Clayton knelt and hugged her neck. "I thought you were injured . . ." Logic finally kicked in. If Rusty was here then what –. Clayton turned. The figure still lay in a heap near the house.

Rusty snarled again, and then turned and ran – heading for home like a racehorse.

"Wait," Clayton tried to yell but something caught in his throat and his voice was no more than a whisper. "There's nothing there . . ."

"Owwwww." A drawn-out mew resonated from the figure.

Clayton staggered backwards. He tripped over something and tumbled onto the ground. The hard earth jarred his tailbone and sharp blades of tussock grass scratched his back.

Get up. Get up and run. Follow Rusty. His legs refused to budge.

He prodded the ground around him and found the hammer. It slipped in his sweaty palms. He wiped his hands on his shorts, grabbed the hammer again and scrambled to his feet.

"Who . . . what are you?" His voice quivered like a tuning fork.

He clasped the hammer tighter and walked towards the house, step by step.

"Answer me. Who are you?"

The air became still and silent. The crunching noise of his shoes intensified.

"It's just a shadow," he reassured himself.

As he walked closer, his conviction wavered. The shadow was the same shape as a fox. It stood, clutching its stomach. Shadows didn't clutch their stomachs. Shadows didn't have a stomach. Or a snout.

Clayton felt as if tiny snakes were slithering in his own stomach. Against his better judgement, he prodded the fox with the hammer's handle.

"Owww," the fox whined.

"Wh . . . what?" Clayton took a step back. His knees shook and he felt that at any moment they would collapse under his weight.

The fox stood up, its body unfurled until it was standing on its two hind legs. The grotesque body of the corpse was so distorted it was hardly recognisable. The fox looked down. "Oh! What a forsaken body this is."

The creature spoke so casually that Clayton almost dropped the hammer in shock. Sure, creatures came to life in his books. But they were books. Maybe this was a book. Maybe it was a dream. A dream from one of his fantasy books. He pinched himself. Surprised at how hard he did it, he winced.

"Clayton, I'm not sure this is the body I would have chosen to occupy."

Unable to tear his eyes away, Clayton only managed to say, "What?" He regained control of his vocal chords. "You called me by my name. How'd you know my name?" He took another step back and thrust the hammer forward.

"I know names, and fears, and dreams." The creature made its way towards Clayton, coming out of the shadows.

Ripped open from the gunshot wound, bloody fur around the fox's exposed skin hung off in chunks. Half its entrails were missing and its torso looked as though it had been scooped out. Its tattered fur was stuck together with dried blood and on its hindquarters was a scabby patch of mange.

The small snakes in Clayton's belly fused into a King Brown, poised and ready to strike. If this was a dream, his fantasy creatures were way off the mark. Mythical creatures were meant to be gracious and mysterious and beautiful; not horrific fox carcasses.

Clayton held the hammer above his head, poised to strike, and staggered backwards. "You're dead. You're twice dead. Dad shot you. You were already dead and Dad shot you."

The leathery skin around its eyes and protruding snout made it look like the personification of death: its eyes dark and sunken. Its skeleton trying to break through the thin veil of skin over its face.

The creature ignored Clayton's gaping stare and walked past him towards the fence. "The portal. You've opened it," it said.

"The boundary gate? That is a portal?"

"Yes. Now is the time. Can't you smell it?"

"Smell what?" Keeping his distance, Clayton followed the creature. The only thing he could smell was rotten flesh. Clayton crept closer to the fox. "Time for what? What do you want?"

"It's not what I want that brings my spirit here. What do you want, Clayton?" asked the fox, pawing at the skin around his belly. It looked as if it was trying to close the gaping hole there.

Clayton clutched his stomach with one hand, struggling not to gag.

"Never mind. Rhetorical question," continued the creature. "You know there is only one thing that can make everything right again. Only one thing can chisel away at the statue that is your father."

"What's that?" Clayton asked.

Standing by the boundary fence, the fox looked across the paddock, up towards the hills and finally the sky. "I can make the water flow upon Paddle Creek Station again. I can make it rain."

CHAPTER 3

Water trickled down from the hills onto the floodplains. Everyone knew that, but the talk of spirits . . . that was something that happened in his books, not in real life. Despite that, and every ounce of logic, there was a dead fox talking to him.

"Who are you?" he asked.

"I told you. I am a spirit," the fox said casually.

Clayton shook his head, shut his eyes, and opened them again. The mangled fox was still there and still standing on its hind legs.

"Do you have a name?" Clayton asked, walking towards the window, away from the spider web.

"Name? What is it with mortals and their desire to label everything?" The creature gazed at Davo's house. "Waringa," it said at last.

"What?"

"You may call me Waringa."

"Couldn't you have used something eerie or magical, like Elfwand, or Sirius, or Falcor? Or something simple?"

"Simple? Is there such a thing?" Waringa walked up alongside Clayton. "Defeating the demon will be far from simple."

"Hmmm?" Clayton looked up to see Waringa had stepped towards him again, close enough to strike. But if he was really some magical spirit who knew what he could do, or from how far away.

"Demons? Making it rain? Do you really expect me to believe that?" he asked.

"Why do you doubt me? You have seen it, have you not?"

"Who?"

"The Red King. You have seen him. In the dust. It brings heat, steals the moisture from the ground and scalds the land."

Clayton recalled the outstretched arm he'd seen in the dust billowing up from the back of his dad's ute. There had been something there. "And this demon will bring back the rain, will it?" asked Clayton.

Waringa shook his head. "No, it is preventing the rain spirits from returning. Once upon a time, they lived in harmony. Blue and grey skies graced the heavens equally. But the Red King grew jealous of the love everyone showed the bringers of rain. The Red King's power intensified and it turned on them, banishing the spirits from the plains."

"Where are these rain spirits now?" Clayton asked.

"They hide in the hills and will not return while the Red King holds power. If you defeat it and free the rain spirits, the water will begin to fall in the hills, run down the slopes, fill the creek and trickle out onto the floodplain of Paddle Creek Station." Waringa pawed at the mange at the base of his tail. "They are waiting to be freed," he continued. "The rains are close."

Clayton peered into the cloudless night sky with its endless shining stars exposed.

"I see you doubt me." Waringa sniffed the air. "Can't you smell it approaching? That sweet dewy scent and earthy essence of rain falling on dust. It is close."

Clayton inhaled deeply. He smelled a hint of Waringa's rotten flesh but nothing else.

"Can you feel it at least?" asked Waringa. "The static in the air. Nature can sense it. The rain spirits speak to the earth and the earth has senses you have long since lost." Waringa pointed a skinny, leathery paw to the soil. "See the ant mounds fortified with coarse sand and stones – temples to hold back the deluge. And above the saltbushes and wattles, flying ants make haste. The rain spirits are telling the world they are ready to be released. They know the warrior has arrived to free them."

"Warrior?" asked Clayton with an intentional hint of sarcasm. "Where is this great warrior? Warriors carry swords and ride dragons, and are brave and strong."

Waringa looked down at Clayton with his sunken eyes.

"What, me? I'm no warrior," Clayton said, averting his gaze from the fox's persistent stare. "I struggle to open a cocky gate. How am I meant to defeat a demon or free these rain spirits?"

Waringa sighed and his furry body shrugged. "I don't know –"

"Fat lot of good you are then. Why am I talking to you? I'm not even sure I am. How can I be talking to a smelly, mange-ridden, dead fox?"

Waringa looked over his shoulder at his tail. "No need for insults. This wasn't my first choice of body. I could have inhabited an emu, or a taipan, or an eagle. Even a wallaby would be more glamorous."

"Why don't you know how to defeat this demon? You seem to know everything else."

"*I* do not know," Waringa said. "But I know someone who does."

Clayton's ears prickled. "Is it Reggie? Dad reckons Reggie is a smart alec and knows everything."

"Adults. They know naught. I speak of the mythical serpent on Paddle Creek."

"Serpent? That's ridiculous. There isn't anything like that here."

"Is that so?" asked Waringa. "There aren't any serpents in the same way there aren't any spirits?"

"Maybe you are a figment of my imagination too." Clayton caught a whiff of the fox's pungent odour. Something that smelled that bad couldn't be just in his head. But a mythical serpent? Clayton imagined something like a Basilisk living in dank, lonely places away from prying eyes, not in the sunburnt denuded landscape here.

"Wouldn't they live in dark hollow places?" Clayton said, half to himself.

"So we need to look for somewhere dark."

Waringa didn't need to say any more. Beside Clayton, the bluestone building compelled him to enter, but at that moment, he couldn't even look at it.

"If you want to free the rain, the serpent is your best chance of finding a way," Waringa said, walking away from him, towards Davo's old house.

Clayton followed at a distance. Stairs creaked as he tiptoed up to the deck.

The two deck chairs sat on the porch as they had always done, although the fabric was a little more frayed than the last time he was here. The chairs jogged memories of Davo's housewarming party a couple of years ago. There had been a barbeque on the deck and Davo and his dad had scuffled half-heartedly over who should be in charge of the tongs. His mum, Nudge and a couple of other local teenagers had fought over who got the privilege of sitting on the only two deckchairs Davo owned. Nudge had jostled in front of everyone else and made a beeline for the chairs only to have the fabric tear under his weight.

"Nice furniture," he'd mocked.

"Don't knock 'em," Davo had said, laughing. "They were on special at the local tip."

Davo ended up insisting that Rusty and Clayton have the only two seats for the night.

But why couldn't Clayton remember anything else? He knew he must've been here before his brother died.

"I can't go in there. Dad won't let me."

"If you cannot do this, I am afraid I don't know how to help you," Waringa said quietly.

Clayton walked to the front door where spiders had made their home in every corner and crevice. The house didn't scare the spiders, so why should it scare him? And his dad never came here so he wouldn't even know he'd been inside.

Clayton took a deep determined breath. The air was fresh with the scent of saltbush and the country breeze. The air was fresh? There was no pungent smell of decay. Clayton turned from the spider mending her web to look at Waringa. He'd gone. He'd vanished without another word.

For a second, Clayton wished the rotting creature were here to help, and then turned his gaze on the heavy wooden door. A brass boar with a doorknocker through its nose sat above the doorhandle.

"Okay," he said to himself. He looked for the old boot where Davo used to hide the spare key. The boot was still there, with holes worn through the toes and heel. What were the chances the key was still here? Only one way to find out. "I can do this," he muttered to himself.

Something creaked behind him. He turned with his back pressed against the door.

"Waringa?" Clayton asked in a hushed voice. The air still smelled fresh. There was no sign of the spirit or anyone else. "The creaking is the house settling," he tried reassuring himself.

He bent down to the boot and found the small skeleton key hiding underneath. As he picked it up, he felt the air sucked from his lungs, and he gasped for breath. He'd bent down to get the key before, but there was darkness and fear attached to that memory. Why? It was just a key. He tried to probe deeper but his mind kept hitting a dark spot, like a locked filing cabinet that refused to open. The more he tried to remember the more his chest hurt and his breathing became sharp and ragged.

Hastily, he returned the key, darted down the stairs, back through the gate and jumped on the quad bike, gasping for breath. He knew in his heart he was no spider. He wasn't made for mending things.

"Everything will be okay. It will rain eventually." Clayton rode in a daze, guided by the headlights. "It has to rain again. Dad and Mum can cope a little longer."

The front wheel of the quad bike jolted in a pothole. The vehicle stalled. Clayton's body lunged forward into the handlebars.

He dismounted the quad, rubbing his ribs. Something shimmered silver on the ground. Clayton walked closer to see a tiny pool of water in the dam reflecting the Moon and stars.

How did he end up here? He'd ridden way off course.

Davo once tried to convince Clayton that two leprechaun brothers buried their stash of silver and gold here, except a great flood washed them and their treasure into the dam.

"The brothers refused to leave their treasures and drowned trying to collect them," Davo had said. "At sunset you sometimes see the eldest brother's ghost trying to toss his gold out of the water, and at night the younger one tries to rescue his silver. But the treasure is trapped down there until the dam dries up completely. So all you see is the golden and silver shimmer as they try to rescue their coins."

Clayton had said that was silly, but Davo always believed in crazy stuff like magic. He might have even believed him about Waringa.

"Don't mock it. It's one of Dad's stories," Davo had said.

"Oh. Therefore it must be true," said Clayton. They both laughed, but Davo's chuckle sounded hollow.

"Dad reckons there's no way he's going to let the cheeky little bugger's ghost out. He's going to make sure it rains." Davo stared intently at the dam with a thoughtful expression. "I ain't ever seen the water this low." His voice changed. "Not even the long dry spell we had before you were born. Dad said you heralded the break of season. You brought a deluge with you when you entered the world. Roads were washed away and everything. I couldn't go to school so I was stuck listening to you bawling all day." Davo plucked a blade of rank wild oats and chewed on its stem. "I haven't been able to prove I can do it on my own yet. Sometimes I wonder whether it'd be easier somewhere else." He'd tossed the blade of grass into the dam. "But, like Dad says, us Hoppers ain't weak."

Clayton punched Davo playfully on his arm.

"Owww."

"Thought you said you weren't weak." Clayton jumped to his feet, avoiding Davo's retaliatory swipe.

"Oh, really. You want to take me on . . . pipsqueak?"

"Pipsqueak!" Clayton grabbed a handful of mud and hurled it at Davo's legs.

"They're my new jeans." Davo raced towards Clayton, but he'd run too close to the edge and his feet sank deep in the mud. He had to take off his shoes to get free. "That's it. You're dead, little bro." He'd grabbed a handful of mud and flung it at Clayton. He ducked and the lump of mud sailed past Clayton and collided with their father, who'd come looking for them. Dad's bellowing voice had rung in Clayton's ears for days afterwards.

Something was buzzing in Clayton's ear, but it wasn't bellowing.

"Clayton." Something shook his arm.

Clayton was lying in the mud. The pool had lost its silver shimmer, as if someone had pulled the plug and let the treasure down the drain.

"Clayton. Come on, mate."

He sat up. Nudge squatted beside him scratching the stubbly beard he'd finally managed to grow.

Sunlight poured across the farm and drenched the paddocks in a bronze light.

"Did I fall asleep?" Clayton asked Nudge.

"Must've done."

"Is Dad worried?" He scrambled to his feet and brushed dirt from his clothes.

Nudge hid his hands in his pockets. "Your mum's been frantic." He wandered to his ute.

Did that mean his dad wasn't? Clayton knew they couldn't have been looking for him long, but surely his dad was a little concerned.

"Come on, mate." Nudge scooted into the driver's seat. "Let's get you home."

The ute was nothing like Dad's. The engine purred whereas his dad's roared, and Nudge's back windscreen was so adorned with stickers from every single outback pub that Clayton couldn't see any dust kick up behind the back wheels.

He shut his eyes and pictured how he'd sneak into his room without making the floor squeak. He could just curl up and pretend he'd been asleep the whole night in his bed. But as Nudge stopped, he scooted out of the ute and ushered Clayton not only to the front door, but into the kitchen.

His mum and dad sat at the table with solemn stares. Nudge took off his Akubra and held it firmly in his hands.

"You okay?" Mum asked in a quiet voice.

"Yeah." Clayton walked to the fridge to get a snack. If he acted as if everything was normal, perhaps his dad wouldn't have a go at him for staying out all night.

The old refrigerator smell poured out of the fridge as he stared at the shelves, pondering why everyone was so quiet. He grabbed an apple, rubbed it on his t-shirt and took a deliberately casual bite.

"Do you want anything while I'm here?" he muttered to his parents with his mouth full.

Mum shook her head and his dad just stared at the table.

Clayton glanced up at Nudge, looking for a sign of why everyone was so sullen.

"Na, I'm fine thanks, buddy," he said. "I should get going anyhow." Nudge snapped his hat back onto his head with a swift flick of the wrist.

"Thought you said you needed to speak to me about something else," Dad said, finally looking up. But he refused to look in Clayton's direction.

Nudge hesitated. "Ummm. Nah, it's fine. It'll wait."

Nudge gave Clayton a smile. There was sympathy and compassion in that smile. But why? He was late, but it couldn't have been *that* much of an issue.

Dad cast his eyes down again as Nudge left the room. The front door shut with an almost inaudible click but the monstrous revving of Nudge's ute filled the silence for a few minutes until his car was out of earshot. Silence resumed, except for the occasional zap of mozzies as they hit the catcher.

"Are you trying to destroy me?" Dad said finally. His eyes never left the table.

Clayton felt as if a tractor ploughed into his guts. Destroy him? "I fell asleep. I wanted to fix –"

"I don't give a shit about that."

"Walt, language," Mum murmured.

"You left the bloody gate open."

"What?" Clayton's mouth fell agape.

"Nudge was going to finish mending the fence this morning and the sheep are roaming through the northern property."

The northern property? It was more than the northern property. It was Davo's.

Dad looked up, eyes ablaze. "Why the bleedin' heck were you even there?"

His father would never believe Clayton if he told him about Waringa. What was he to say? What could he say? Instead, he shrugged.

"I thought I told you not to go near that place. This is just what I need. Now I have to pay Nudge to round-up the sheep tomorrow. How am I meant to pay him? Even if by some miracle money actually grew on trees, do you see many trees around Paddle Creek?"

Clayton let his dad finish ranting.

Mum stared at the table. Say something, Clayton thought. Tell Dad he should be worried about me.

She stood up and looked at her husband. For a second, it appeared as though his mum might have heard his thoughts, but then she turned away. "I should go fold the laundry," she said.

Again? "Why don't *you* go round them up?" Clayton blurted to his dad.

Mum turned midstride and glared at Clayton with a frown that made him bite his tongue.

"We can round them up," Clayton said. "We can all go and round them up. Or we could leave them there." His voice lost its resolve as he said the last part. His dad didn't acknowledge his outburst and his mum might have well said nothing.

"I'll cook a late breakfast after I've folded the laundry. Do you want to help me, Clayton, sweetie?"

He ignored her and focused on his dad. "How do you know it was me? Maybe Nudge forgot to shut the gate. Why'd you assume —"

"Nudge isn't a flaming idiot. *He* wouldn't do that to me."

It felt like his dad dragged a prickle chain across his soul, ripped it up and churned his hope deep into the earth. A lump grew in the back of his throat and tears threatened. Clayton stormed to his room and slammed the door. A soft whimper came from his bed as he turned on the lights. Rusty lay with her paw rested over her eyes, whether trying to block out the light or the noise, Clayton wasn't sure. Clayton lay down next to the kelpie and followed her lead, putting the pillow over his head, blocking out the light, the noise and reality.

CHAPTER 4

Chatter and a slobbering tongue woke Clayton from a dreamless sleep. Rusty sat back as soon as Clayton coaxed his head from the soft pillow.

"How long were we asleep, girl?" he asked, pushing Rusty's wet tongue away from his face.

As he staggered out of bed, raised voices drifted through the open door.

"You can't splurge like this," he heard his mum say. "There are leftovers for tea."

"I shouldn't have yelled, Em." Dad's voice started to rise, frustrated.

"Sure, I get that, but –" Mum had started to raise her voice.

Don't start yelling, Clayton prayed as he hurried to the kitchen, thumping his feet to ensure they heard him coming and would stop.

"But that's not how you fix –"

"Clayton," Mum said as if he'd been gone for days. "You missed lunch. I didn't want to wake you. You looked so tired." She pulled out a chair at the table. "Sit. I'll get you some leftovers."

"Forget that," Dad said. "We'll get a proper man's feed at the pub."

Mum gritted her teeth.

"Got something for you. You can show this off at the pub." Dad tapped a massive cardboard box on the table with his stubby finger. "Go on, mate. Open it."

Clayton looked at the package sitting on the kitchen table between them and peered up at his dad. "What's it for?"

"Just a small gift for my little bronco." Dad sat down and drummed his fingers on the table like an impatient child.

"What is it?"

"'What's it for? What is it?' Just open her." For once, there was a hint of excitement in Dad's voice.

Clayton picked at the packing tape. It came off in small strips.

"Here." Dad grabbed a steak knife and sliced down the middle of the packing tape with one quick stroke. "Go on."

Clayton pulled back the flaps of the box. Layers of foam covered whatever was inside. Given the amount of packaging, it was unlikely to be the books he said he wanted recently.

"Gor, you're slower than a ewe in a sandstorm." Dad ripped out the packaging and threw it on the floor, much to Rusty's delight. "Git out of there, girl." He nudged the kelpie away from the wrapping.

Clayton peered into the box. An Akubra sat in a bed of polystyrene balls.

"It's real felt." Dad lifted the hat out of the box and ran his finger around the brim. "Here, try it on."

"Walt!" Mum sighed.

"He can't go around wearing that old bucket hat forever. It's worn and it makes him look like a bleedin' fisherman."

"What's wrong my fishing hat? It was a present from –"

"Just try it," interrupted Mum, well aware that Davo gave it to him.

"This old thing?" His Dad plucked Clayton's bucket hat from the table and tossed it towards Rusty. "Don't be daft."

Davo gave it to me. As much as Clayton tried, the words wouldn't escape his lips. "Thanks," he muttered instead and put on the Akubra. It hung down over his eyes.

He pushed it back and caught his reflection in the microwave door. The brim was so wide it looked like an umbrella sprouting from his head. "Isn't it a bit big?"

"She'll be right. You'll grow into it."

Clayton felt like a rodeo clown, but there was a trace of a smile on his dad's face. He missed that smile so much.

Dad wiped his hands on his dusty work pants. "Well, I'll go wash up for tea. Back in a moment."

As soon as Dad left, Clayton turned to his mum. "It looks ridiculous," he whispered.

"It just looks awkward because it's new. Give it time."

Clayton removed the Akubra, placed it carefully on the table and put the empty box on the floor.

"There was nothing wrong with my other hat," he said.

"Here." Mum handed Clayton the Akubra.

He put it back on reluctantly. If there was any chance a change of hat would bring life back to his dad, he'd put up with looking like a mushroom.

From under the wide brim of his Akubra, Clayton stared out the window as the ute rattled down the dirt road towards town. The five o'clock shadow of chewed saltbush ran for kilometres as they drove across their property, then Kallangabar station and the lane of bare dirt that was the airstrip. Further down the road, Reggie's paddocks looked like they'd been shaved bald. His tractor cruised across one, dragging a prickle chain behind it, much to the satisfaction of the cockatoos and corellas digging their beaks into the churned-up soil.

"I can't believe he's bloody well fallowing it," Dad said. "It's just dust. Bloody idiot."

"Language, Walt," whispered Mum.

Dad ignored her. "Who let that hobby farmer out of the stockades is anyone's guess."

"Language, Dad," whispered Clayton.

"What you on about, boy?" Dad looked across at Clayton.

"*Hobby* farmer?" Clayton smiled, hoping it would rub off on his dad. "Just because he's got less than a hundred hectares is no reason for insults."

"Hah!" Dad snorted a half-chuckle. His eyes didn't share the joke, but it was a start.

Clayton gazed back out the window as they turned off the dirt track onto the bitumen. The cracked and pot-holed surface of the main road through town didn't provide a much smoother ride. The lone streetlight flickered on as the skies darkened with dusk, illuminating the general store, the shed of the Country Fire Service, and the two old houses along the main drag. The old shed that was the pub sat on the corner. The tin roof had signs of rust, and above it, the trees tried desperately to hold onto their withered limbs, heavy with copper coloured mistletoe and leaves that were a sickly shade of khaki. It was as if they no longer had the strength to hold their arms upright.

Clayton scrambled out of the car the instant Dad pulled into the car park, but it took Mum a while to persuade Dad the pub was still a good idea.

At the front door, the pin-board's posters advertised part-time cleaning services, gardening, and farmhands. Their tear-off slips pleaded to be taken. The sign above the door should have read "Hawk's Hotel" but the faded red lettering was barely visible and in desperate need of a fresh coat of paint.

They used to come here for Sunday roasts. Clayton had always loved the pub: the run-down tin shed with exposed rafters and wine barrels for tables. He even loved its old motley carpet and the stale cigarette smell that clung to the woodwork. He remembered running bare foot across the floor when he was younger, the carpet slightly sticky underfoot. He'd play 8-ball – Davo and him against Dad. Although their father always won, he hadn't cared. It didn't even matter that he couldn't reach the table. Davo would lift him up so Clayton could take the shot. Of course, Dad would complain that pub rules stated one foot must always be on the floor, but Davo always came to his defence. "His foot is my foot and my foot is his foot." He'd point to the ground. "We're touching the floor."

Pub rules—there were so many of them. The most important being that life's troubles were left at the door.

But as Clayton and his family entered the pub now, there was no pool table, no sticky carpet, just souls slumped over schooners and an eerie silence.

As Dad led the way to the bar, the silence seemed to deepen. Clayton heard the occasional slurp of beer and his mum sighed deeply.

"Walt. Emily." The bartender greeted them with forced casualness. "Long time no see. Clay, matey." The bartender lifted Clayton's new Akubra and ruffled his hair.

"Hi," Clayton muttered, flattening his hair so it sat straight again.

Dad grunted in acknowledgment. "Hawksey, what d'ya know?"

"Things are ticking along. Here for a counter-meal?" Hawksey asked.

Dad nodded.

Clayton perched himself on a bar stool and gazed at the adults. He didn't understand them. During school, his teacher would always ask the kids on the stations how they were, instead of these absurd greetings of "what do you know" and "long time no see".

Ask Dad how he is today. Ask him how he's been since he was last here with the whole family, before Davo died. Ask him how he was when he discharged a whole round of ammo on the sky because it didn't rain.

The publican asked nothing of the sort, instead he handed them menus.

"Three rare steaks," Dad said without even looking at his menu. He turned to Clayton. "You want chips or veggies?"

Clayton looked up at his dad quizzically. Did he really not know him at all?

"Silly question," Dad said, "chips it is."

"I want Thai Beef Salad," corrected Clayton.

"What you on about? You don't want bleeding rabbit food. You need some meat on your bones."

"I don't want steak."

"Don't be absurd. You used to love steak sandwiches," said Dad.

Clayton tried to shake his head, but it felt as if something was bracing his neck. Instead, he swallowed and drilled holes in the bar counter with his eyes and managed to mutter, "No I didn't."

"Sure you did. We used to come here after we'd been to feed the cattle on hot days and you'd always have a steak sanga. Onion, beetroot and extra chips."

That was Davo, thought Clayton. He looked at his mum for support, but she hadn't said a word since they entered. The television hanging above the bar had diverted her attention. It wasn't even anything interesting. Football. She hated football. Blue and green lights cast shadows across her eyes.

"Mum, can't I have a salad?" asked Clayton.

"Clayton, sweetie, just this once have a steak." Her voice cracked and she avoided looking at him. "It won't hurt you." She stood abruptly and left the front bar, leaving him sitting next to Dad, surrounded by the local farmers and yet feeling invisible and alone.

The publican gave Clayton a brief look as if asking for his approval. "Three steaks it is. You want drinks?"

"Yeah, usual. Shandy for Em, I'll have a pint and Clay'll have a lemonade," said Dad.

Lemonade? Clayton wanted to tell the barman he wanted an orange juice, but he couldn't bring himself to correct Dad again.

Hawksey hurried off and the silence resumed as they waited for their meals and his mum to return. Something must've set off memories of Davo. It could be the football. Clayton remembered his brother had played for a while. He'd given it up when he got his own land though, saying he wanted to put all his energy into his farm. *At least Mum cares*, thought Clayton. *Unlike Dad, who's pretending Davo never existed.*

A thud resonated from the other side of the room as a dart pierced the dartboard hanging beside the old jukebox.

"What do you think, Dad?" asked Clayton, cocking his head in the dartboard's direction. "Can we have a game?"

"Maybe later," Dad mumbled.

"You used to play all the time. It'd be good—"

"Later." Dad massaged his temples.

Clayton noticed the people sitting along the bar were staring at him and the stares seemed to heighten Dad's silence. "I wouldn't mind a game," Clayton said, "but I don't know how to throw them."

"Don't let Walter near those things."

Clayton turned to see Nudge standing behind them. "In his hands, they're a lethal weapon," he continued.

"Nudge!" Walter stood and slapped him on the back. Although he welcomed Nudge with a friendly gesture, there was no denying the frown lingering in his eyes.

"You see Reggie bleedin' well fallowed his paddock?" Dad finally said. "Bit optimistic, don't you think?"

"If you work her, she'll come." Nudge beamed a wicked grin and held his hands up, gesturing to the sky.

"*Maybe* this is the year," said Dad sceptically. "I'd like to think this'll be the season she breaks. I admit I do have a feeling in my bones."

"You sure that ain't just your arthritis?" asked Nudge.

"Cut that cheek out. Come on, son. I'll shout you a beer."

'*Son*'. The word stung. Clayton peered so closely at his soft drink the bubbles fizzed up his nose.

"That's okay." Nudge backed away from the bar a pace.

"Come on, just a quick one." Dad took a long deep draught that more-or-less emptied the glass. "Consider it down payment for some more work."

"Walt, I can't accept a free beer."

"I know I still owe you money, but I've got a water trough that needs fixing and I promise I'll sort you out soon as we get back on our feet."

"Walt, I'm sorry. I really can't."

"Don't be daft, course you can. Shouldn't be hard. Just probably need to replace a couple of valves. I'd do it but—"

"Walt, I've accepted another job."

Clayton looked up at his father's shrunken face.

"I'm sorry, Walt." Nudge looked down, his Akubra shadowing his eyes. "But they're offering jobs at the new mine up north and—"

"Mining?"

"They need workers and the pay's good."

"Don't be daft. You're meant to be on the land, not down a stinking hole. I know work's been slow, but once we get a decent rain things'll pick up and we'll be able to afford to pay the farmhands more."

"Sorry, Walt. It's time I moved on. And there's too many memories here."

"You can't leave. Who do I have left to help?"

A lump, like dry sand, formed in the back of Clayton's throat. He took a sip of lemonade but it turned the sand into mud, cloying the back of his throat. *I'm still here*, he thought from underneath his invisibility cloak.

The tin roof rattled as a gust of wind roared outside. The door to the bar swung open and leaves skittled inside on a whiff of dust.

Clayton wandered to the front door and peered outside. It was dark but the streetlight shone on a thick haze sweeping down the road. Was the Red King coasting the pub, waiting for them to emerge? Wind wafted in his face and he tasted the bitterness of dust.

"Clayton!" his mum called out.

He turned back to the bar.

Mum had returned, and Hawksey carried out their meals.

"Tea's ready," she said.

Clayton gazed back outside but the sky was clear again. He shut the door and strolled back to the bar to find three bleeding raw steaks.

Behind a fresh coat of makeup, Mum's cheeks were streaked red with tears and looked as raw as the meat.

"This looks nice, Hawksey," she said, sitting down on her bar stool.

Hawksey acknowledged her with a nod.

"Doesn't this look nice?" she asked Clayton as he sat in front of his meal.

"Hmmm, thanks," he mumbled in Hawksey's direction and nibbled at the greasy, limp fries.

"Well, this is nice," Mum said, the cheerfulness in her voice in contradiction to her tear-stained faced.

"Hawksey," said Nudge trying to sound cheerful and pretend he didn't just deal Walter a blow. "If my tab is still only in double figures, can you get me the barramundi?"

When Nudge headed up north, all the smiles and laughter and chatter would leave with him. He was leaving Clayton alone with his dad's brittle statue and his mum's broken soul. He was leaving, Davo had left, and where was Waringa?

A *ping* rang out on the tin roof, stopping Hawksey from taking Nudge's order. Dad put down his steak knife. Mum looked up at the ceiling. Another metallic *ping* echoed on the roof. The chime seemed to last for an eternity.

"It's only a couple of drops. Don't get too excited," mumbled Dad to no one in particular.

Several pings rang out at once. Dad looked up. Everyone stared at the ceiling as if expecting rain to fall from the rafters. The chimes fell in a rhythmical pattern: pitter-patter like possums were tap dancing on the roof.

When the wind gusted at home, the roof would rumble as if it were about to take off, but this sound was soothing and melodic.

The pitter-patter turned to rapid beats. And they were loud. Perhaps loud enough to be hail.

An old man at the other end of the bar stood up and walked towards the door. Nudge followed. There was a mass exodus of adults towards the door then, as though the pied piper was playing a hypnotic song outside.

Clayton followed his parents as the patrons spilled onto the main road.

Outside, the night air bristled with electricity, but the sky was clear of clouds. The stars gleamed brightly against the night sky.

People began to filter back inside. Clayton watched his dad continue to stare up at the sky. All of a sudden, Dad started laughing.

Nudge approached and tapped his shoulder. "You okay?"

Dad ripped his arm away from Nudge. "Go on, piss off then. Go dig your holes."

"Walt?" asked Nudge looking as stunned as Clayton felt.

"You're too weak for this place. You're all weak." Dad turned to the publican and patrons gathering at the door.

Mum stood in the doorway, looking on with wide eyes. Everyone looked. No one spoke.

"I know things are tough," Nudge began. "With everything that has happened—"

"*He* was weak too," Dad said.

Nudge swung his fist at Dad, but he sidestepped the blow. "How dare you!" said Nudge.

Clayton watched on helpless as the pub seemed to drift into a time warp with events unfolding in slow motion.

Mum sobbed and clutched the doorframe. There was no questioning who they were arguing about. The other patrons gave her space. They didn't comment or criticise or help. They just stood there or wandered back inside to drown in their beers.

"How many times did he try to talk to you?" Nudge asked. "But of course you're too manly to listen to anything he had to say."

Dad let his fist fly. It smacked Nudge in the face, knocking him over and sending his Akubra flying onto the street.

Clayton glanced between his mum and dad and Nudge sitting on the ground clutching his nose. He wanted to stop them, but his legs were shaking. His dad just punched someone. Dad had never hit anyone before. He'd hit a lot of farming equipment when it was uncooperative, but never a person. And it wasn't just any person – it was Nudge.

"Walter!" Mum called from the front door.

There were men running from the pub towards Dad. His dad swung his fist again as a burly looking bloke approached. He missed and stumbled.

"You're all piss weak. Weak as shit." Dad pulled himself erect. Turning his back on the men he stormed down the street.

The men let him go and helped Nudge to his feet.

Clayton wanted to run after Dad. He wanted to run to Mum or to Nudge. Instead, he backed away slowly.

He slunk off into the car park, leaned against Dad's ute and tried to clear his head. There was too much in there, vague thoughts and feelings and emotions that refused to leave him alone. Clayton clasped his head in his hands, trying to block out the world and slumped down next to the car. He rested his back against the tyres. Whether he sat there for a long time or the world was still stuck in slow motion, Clayton couldn't tell, but the melodic chiming returned and jolted him to his feet. He extended his hand to the sky, but no raindrops cooled his palm.

In between the pitter-patter, a deep growl resonated from under the gum trees.

With just a sliver of moon shining above and the lights glowing dimly from inside the pub, Clayton could barely make out his surroundings. But the lights illuminated glaring eyes in the shrubbery.

Clayton got to his feet, back pressed against his dad's ute and called into the dark, "Hello?"

Two yellow eyes shone in midair. Shrubs rustled, the eyes floating forwards until the pub lights shone on fur and a snout.

Waringa's eyes didn't look nearly as sunken and dark as they had last night, and the leathery skin looked as if it had received a good dose of Botox. Clayton didn't know how it was possible, but the fox looked taller too.

"I have tried to fix up this vessel," said the fox, looking down at its body, "but I have not had have much success."

Clayton followed its gaze. The fox had stitched the gaping hole in its stomach with pink baling twine, it poked through the fur and skin. What the creature had used to sew it, Clayton hated to think. The skin was still red and raw and stretched tight with a crosshatched pattern of stitches straddling the wound.

"Does it hurt?" asked Clayton.

"Pain? Pain is subjective. You can block out pain quite easily. You can easily choose to forget. Don't *you* think?"

"Huh?" Clayton tried to rip his eyes away from the wound. The stitching was more disturbing than the gaping hole he'd seen last night. The sight made him feel queasy and he suddenly remembered he was talking to a dead fox who thought it was a spirit. He felt light-headed and leaned against the ute to steady himself.

"What is that growing from your head?" asked Waringa.

"Oh, this." Clayton quickly removed the Akubra. "Dad gave it to me."

"It looks ridiculous on you. Mortals. They have the fashion sense of a hermit crab."

Clayton was going to point out that the spirit inhabited a carcass stitched together with pink baling twine, but he let the fashion advice slide.

"The hat makes Dad happy."

"Makes him happy?" mimicked Waringa. "Do you think warriors win battles by appeasing people?"

Waringa's snout was inches from Clayton's eyes. "You look troubled," the fox said. "Do not fret about the serpent. I've discovered another myth that might help." Waringa held up a clenched paw and for a second Clayton thought the spirit was going to punch him, but he opened his paw, revealing gumnuts.

Clayton shrugged. "What're they for? Are you going to plant them and climb up a magic gumtree to the sky and make it rain?"

"What poppycock have you been reading?" asked Waringa. The fox hurled the gumnuts at the roof.

"What are you doing?"

Waringa bent down and scraped through the dirt of the car park to find more gumnuts. "Provocation," he said, hurling another seed. It tinkled as it hit the tin roof.

"Stop that!" Clayton yelled. "It'll upset Dad."

"We'll use the same tactic to antagonise the Red King and bring it out of hiding. Face the demon head-on," continued Waringa, ignoring Clayton's pleas.

"With gumnuts?" mocked Clayton.

"Don't be absurd. There is a myth of a weapon the Red King buried under the earth covered in layers of his dust. If the Red King fears this weapon so much as to hide it, it may prove useful and bring the demon out of hiding."

"Where is this weapon?" asked Clayton, a glimpse of hope spreading through him.

"Somewhere out there." Waringa turned his head in the direction of Paddle Creek Station.

"That's not particularly useful. The station is huge."

"It is either that or seek advice from the serpent."

"You already got me into trouble with the gate. I don't want to upset Dad by going into Davo's house."

"How do you intend to fix things then?" Waringa picked up another handful and drew back his arm to throw them. Clayton pushed the fox's paw and the gumnuts scattered across the car park. Waringa took a step backwards towards the shrubs. "Some things cannot be fixed with baling twine and silly hats. If you want to fight and bring back rain, you may have to upset the apple-cart."

"Clayton!" Mum yelled.

Clayton turned to see her walking out of the pub, her puffy red eyes were visible even in the dim light.

"Are you going to eat your meal?" she asked.

Clayton turned back to Waringa, surprised she hadn't spotted him, but he had disappeared. Only amber eyes remained, slinking into the undergrowth.

"Your steak's getting cold." Mum placed a hand on his shoulder. "Come on. You can eat some for your dad. He's just gone for a walk."

Clayton looked up at his mum; her eyes were focused in the direction Dad had stormed off.

"You know, that pub is really stuffy and your dad needed some fresh air," she said. "But he'll be back soon."

Squaring his shoulders under his mum's hand, Clayton nodded and took a deep breath. Mum couldn't help him win this battle. He'd eat his steak. Then he'd fight.

CHAPTER 5

Sulphur-crested cockatoos welcomed dawn with high-pitched squawks. Rusty leaped up from where she was sprawled on the end of the bed and scratched at the window. Clayton sat up and opened the blinds so Rusty could gaze longingly at the white birds descending onto the Hills Hoist.

The morning sun slinked through the window, meandered across the floorboard, skittered up the bookcase, and rested its warm gaze upon the new Akubra hanging on the back of the door. Clayton dragged a drooling Rusty from the window and shut the blinds, casting shadows onto his hat. Last night, he'd been determined to find the weapon and bring the Red King out of hiding, but in the light of day things didn't seem so simple. If the weapon *was* under layers of dust it would mean digging up the paddocks to find it. Wombats were already digging warrens all over the place. Surely, Dad wouldn't appreciate any more holes.

Rusty panted her warm breath in Clayton's ear.

"I know, I know. We gotta find it for Dad."

The kelpie scratched at Clayton's pillow.

"There's nothing buried under my pillow." Clayton threw on a pair of cut-off jeans and a t-shirt. "Come on, girl."

Rusty jumped off the bed and padded behind Clayton. Infomercials droned softly in the lounge room, and Dad sat hunched on the couch. In the white light from the TV, his dad looked like a marble effigy.

"Are you okay?" asked Clayton.

"Hmmm?" His dad stole his eyes away from the television and glanced at Clayton. "Yeah, fine." The anger that had surfaced last night had vanished.

"Maybe today we could drive south and drop a line in Macka's dam," suggested Clayton. "Apparently he's still got a bit of water."

"Dunno. It's a long drive and I got work to do."

"Can I help?"

Dad took a sip from a mug of coffee in his hands and screwed up his eyes. "I have to check the water trough in the samphire paddock and fix the generator and run out a couple of bales for the sheep. I don't have time to dilly-dally around."

Clayton's determination solidified. Helping Dad around the farm obviously wasn't going to make him happy but freeing the rain spirits might.

"I can take hay to the sheep." The hay shed was as good a place as any to begin searching for the Red King's weapon, as the demon had been hanging around there yesterday.

"What you gonna do, carry them out there?" Dad placed his mug on the coffee table and turned back to Clayton. "You ain't taking the ute and I need the tractor later to do some more ripping."

"I can take the old tractor." Clayton didn't have the guts to call it Davo's tractor, not when he finally had Dad on his side. "It's just sitting —"

"Take the quad and hook the tipping trailer up to it."

"But I know how to drive the tractor."

"Perhaps I should come out with you. I'd get it done quicker —"

"No, it's fine. I got this. I'll use the quad." Clayton went to leave.

"Hang on, matey."

Clayton turned, hoping Dad hadn't changed his mind.

"Aren't you forgetting something?"

Clayton looked sheepish. "Am I?"

"It's going to be hot. Hat?"

"Right," said Clayton, guessing Dad didn't mean his fishing hat.

Clayton scooted back into his room, grabbed the Akubra and returned to see Rusty licking the television screen.

"Take her with you." Dad threw a cushion at Rusty. She gnawed on it in front of the telly instead of moving. "She'll slow me down."

"Come on, girl," said Clayton.

Rusty ran up to Dad and leaped onto the lounge suite.

"She likes being with you," said Clayton.

"Yeah, well, I like doing my work without being slobbered on by a disobedient mutt."

She's no mutt. She's Davo's. Clayton picked up the cushion and wiggled it enticingly. "Rusty, down!"

She scampered up to Clayton and pawed at the cushion. "Come on, girl." He turned to leave.

"Oi! You got your head on straight today?"

Please don't change your mind, thought Clayton, holding his breath.

"Don't you need the keys to the quad?" Dad asked.

"No, there's —" Clayton instantly remembered the key under the shed's workbench was Davo's secret. "Oh, yeah. Whoops," he said, trying to sound sincere.

Dad pushed himself off the couch with a drawn-out groan and wandered across the lounge room to the glass cabinet. He grabbed the small key on top of it, unlocked the cabinet, and reached beyond the rifle to several keys hanging on hooks.

Dad took the key to the quad. "Here."

Clayton grabbed the key and led Rusty outside before his dad said anything else.

By the time he made it to the hay sheds, the sun was peeking above the trees with abrasive heat.

Assuming the quad bike needed fuel, he grabbed the jerry can from the bench.

"Where's the funnel?" Clayton mumbled to himself. He scanned the mess covering the shed floor. Beyond the collection of spinning jennies, tractor parts and other farming equipment, new hay bales towered towards the ceiling like a pyramid. At the far end of the shed, Davo's tractor collected dust and spider webs.

Clayton gave up trying to find the funnel and walked around the header, which hadn't been used for ages, to the quad. He unscrewed the fuel cap and gently tipped the jerry can, resting it against his hip to keep the heavy container steady and not slop the petrol over the sides. Dad was always on about keeping the shed clean, although looking over the mess of tools it seemed a bit hypocritical.

Something hit the back of his knee, jolting the jerry can from the lip of the fuel tank.

"Rusty!" he yelled as the fuel trickled down his arm and leg.

She raced up to Davo's tractor, peed next to the massive rear tyre and jumped through the open door onto the passenger seat.

"Not today," said Clayton. "We're taking the quad."

Rusty got up, walked in circles on the seat and lay down again.

"Rusty, get down!"

She lifted her head in Clayton's direction but then nestled her snout on the seat again.

"Come on," he coaxed. "Come on, girl."

Clayton gave up when she didn't respond. He grabbed a rag and mopped up the fuel from his limbs and side of the quad.

"Be like that then." Clayton hooked up the trailer attachment onto the quad, climbed up the tower of bales and pushed off the top five, letting them tumble to the ground. He made his way back down, taking care not to topple the remaining haystack.

With a loop of twine in each hand and straining his back, he lugged the hay bales onto the trailer. Somehow, Davo used to do this with one hand like Dad did.

He started the quad, and at the sound of the motor whirring into action Rusty jumped from the tractor and perched herself on top of the bales before Clayton managed to back out of the shed.

"Oh, I almost forgot." Clayton jumped off the quad again and dashed across the shed. "Why didn't you remind me?"

Rusty lifted her head, barked, and darted over to the tractor.

"No, not that." Clayton reached for the shovel suspended by a hook above the workbench. "Unless you plan on digging for me, I guess I need this." He popped it down the side of the trailer next to the bales and called to Rusty. She sniffed the tractor. Her determination to go on Davo's tractor made it difficult for Clayton to swallow. Davo loved that tractor. Davo used to let him sit on the bucket attachment when he was doing excavation around the paddocks. Dad would've had a fit if he'd known.

Clayton gave up coaxing Rusty to join him, got back on the quad and headed out across the paddock, keeping an eye behind him for Rusty.

Realising she'd been left alone, she barked furiously and pelted towards the quad bike. Clayton slowed down so she could catch up.

"You want to get up?"

Rusty leaped onto Clayton's lap and licked his ear.

"Not on my lap. On the trailer!"

Rusty ignored his instructions, circled twice on Clayton's lap, her paws digging into his thighs, before sitting down.

Clayton gazed over the top of her head. "Fine. You can sit there if you help me dig."

He drove to the internal fence north of the shed. The quad grumbled as it rattled across a cattle grid and onto the ochre soil.

The sheep sensed his presence and a beige trail trotted behind him kicking up dust.

Clayton stopped and turned the engine off. "Come on, girl. Off you get."

Rusty looked up at him and panted.

"Down." He gave her a nudge.

She jumped down and raced across the paddock towards a few dozen cockatoos and corellas perched on the fence. They took flight and the mass of white wings shimmered silver in the light like fish scales.

Clayton let Rusty play while he snapped the baling twine with the shovel and scattered the hay onto the ground in a long trail.

The sheep billowed dust from their hooves as they bustled for position among the feed strewn on the dry ground.

Clayton looked out across the flat land. Besides the hills to the north, there didn't seem to be any end to the paddocks. It was as if the red land bled into the sky.

Somewhere under the surface was a weapon that *might* help. It was little to go on.

Maybe if the sheep shuffled along the earth enough, their hooves would kick the dirt away and uncover the weapon. The thought didn't fill him with confidence, but he wasn't going to find it if he didn't try.

"I guess here is as good a place as any," he said, taking the shovel and moving away from the mass of sheep.

Although the soil was richer here, the shovel only made a tiny indent in the ground and the impact sent a huge jolt to his elbows.

Around him, the air and ground heated up and wind stirred. Content with their feed, the sheep wandered off to the western side of the paddock where a few wattles cast dappled shade. A tiny trail of dust drifted into the air behind them. Oblivious to the heat, Rusty raced across the dry plains chasing any bird that dared to land.

Clayton tried digging in the sliver of shade the quad bike and trailer cast, but as the sun rose higher, the shadows shrank and the heat bore down on him. He wiped beads of sweat from his brow with the bottom of his t-shirt. The wind picked up speed and cooled him, but the shade of distant bushes beckoned.

"Rusty. Here, girl. We're going to try over there." Clayton jumped back in the quad and started the ignition. Within seconds, Rusty bounded across the paddock and onto his lap. "Jump." He pointed to the trailer.

Rusty stared at him with big eyes. "No. Trailer." He nudged Rusty until she leaped into the back.

The wind whipped Clayton's t-shirt against his skin as he drove down the worn track towards the trees.

A wave of pale pink dust swept over the ochre ground like mist over water. It funnelled across the track near a gap in the western fence, and Clayton hit the brakes before colliding with the dust storm.

It's just dirt, he thought.

The channel of dust billowed upwards into a tall pillar and crept along the track towards Clayton.

Just a change in the wind direction. The mass of dust sped up and rolled towards him. Finger-like tendrils extended in his direction as if the dusty column were clawing at the earth to pull itself forward.

With no one around to help, Clayton lost his nerve: he turned the quad around and headed back towards the shelter of the shed. Sand and small stones hit the back of his neck and arms. He looked over his shoulder and got a mouthful of dust. A hollow chuckle echoed behind him. Wind tore his Akubra from his head and spun it across the paddock.

Clasping the accelerators tightly on the handlebars, he tore along the track. The stones and dust ceased their attack on his skin. Clayton turned to see the mountain of dust lunging behind.

The quad bike jolted to a stop and lurched forward as he veered off the track into a large bluebush. The engine grumbled and stalled.

"Not now." Clayton turned the key. The quad spluttered. "Come on, you rusted clap bucket."

The quad spluttered with ragged grunts and groans and then stopped completely.

"Come on, come on." Pleading did little to make it cooperate.

Behind him, the dust had caught up. Clayton deserted the quad and pelted for the shed. The dusty mass of the Red King bombarded him with twigs and straw that whipped against his bare legs. It felt like someone was flicking him with a wet towel. Dad and Davo used to have towel fights all the time, and Rusty would . . . Rusty. Clayton looked around him. All the way to the horizon, there was nothing but hazy sky and dust smothering every inch of the paddock like a blanket.

CHAPTER 6

"Rusty!" Clayton ran back, grains of sand stinging his eyes. The surrounding haze flowed inwards, as if folding in on itself, until it combined into a single mass on the northern side of the paddock. As the rest of the sky cleared, Clayton spotted Rusty cowering in the trailer, ears flat on her head.

"Rusty, come here!" Clayton yelled, but he could barely hear his own voice against the whistling of the wind.

The dust cloud grew and floated closer. Tendrils wafted towards the trailer and formed stumps like arms.

"No!" Clayton sprinted towards the quad.

Sand grains pinged against the side of the metal trailer and stung his bare legs. He jumped into the trailer and grabbed Rusty's collar.

"Come on, girl." He tried to say it calmly, but his fear betrayed him and his voice crackled. He jumped out of the trailer, trying to coax the kelpie to follow.

Rusty placed her paws on the edge of the trailer but wind lashed about them and she slunk down again. The dust gained speed, eddying around saltbushes. It picked up dirt from the earth and pulled it towards its body like a magnet attracted paperclips. Clayton craned his neck to look up at the Red King towering high into the sky. Grabbing Rusty in his arms, he grunted and managed to lift her out of the trailer. Placing her on the ground, he prayed she'd follow if he started to run.

"Come on." He ran a few paces and she followed.

The hard ground shuddered through his legs as he ran. He glanced back to make sure Rusty was still on his heels and kept running.

Behind him, the Red King's arms pounded the ground, sending dust into the air and turning the sky pink.

The air closed in on Clayton. The bitterness hit the back of his throat, making him gag.

Squinting through the red haze, he saw the gap in the fence was close. He looked over his shoulder. Cheekbones and a long nose protruded from the mass of dust and an indented mouth smiled maliciously.

Clayton's foot hit the metal bar of the cattle grid and, before he knew it, he lost his balance. His foot slid into a gap and his ankle bone hit the metal bar, sending a sharp pang down his legs.

Rusty stopped short of the cattle grid.

"Here . . . girl." Out of breath, Clayton choked on the words.

She stood panting, her tongue lolling with drool, ignorant to the demon approaching behind.

"Rusty, here!" Clayton tugged on his foot trapped in the cattle grid. "Behind you!"

Rusty turned, and seeing the demon, snarled and lurched forward.

"No! Rusty, heel!" His command fell on deaf ears. Rusty tore off like a V8 towards the demon until the dust concealed her from sight. "Please, Rusty!" Clayton tugged at his foot again.

A cackling voice echoed through the haze. "If cattle grids trip you up, how do you expect to defeat me?" The haze in front of him condensed, becoming thicker.

Clayton reached between the bars of the cattle grid, undid his laces, took off his shoe and slipped his foot through the bars.

He glanced up to see the face of the demon staring down at him, arms reaching.

Barking and howling echoed through the haze.

"Rusty!" The side of Clayton's ankle throbbed, but there was no time to worry about the injury now, not when Davo's dog was out there.

A deep chuckle responded, drowning out Rusty's yelps and howls in the distance. "Don't try to thwart my dominion. It is my time to rule." Now fully formed, the demon floated towards him, moving without legs. The arms lashed about like tentacles and dust swirled around its body. An image of the demon burying him under layers of dust, like it had done to the weapon, filtered into Clayton's mind: buried alive in the middle of the paddock where no one would ever find him. He shuddered at the thought.

The demon drifted backwards, and its face turned in Rusty's direction.

"Rusty, run!" He reached down, clasped his shoelaces and pulled his shoe out of the cattle grid.

"Leave her alone!" He flung the shoe with as much strength as he could muster. It connected with the demon's temple. The demon grew thinner and tiny whiffs of dust dispersed into the air from its head.

Clayton searched desperately for a stone, a stick or anything that might have more of an impact. But there was nothing to use as a weapon.

When he looked back up, the dust had merged again, reforming facial features and arms.

He knew he should run, he should ignore his throbbing ankle and run to Rusty. But the thought of running towards the demon made his chest tighten. He shuffled over the cattle grid a few inches.

The movement caught the demon's attention and it turned back to face Clayton.

"Get away from there!" There was a hint of fear in the demon's voice, but why?

A dusty gale collided with Clayton, knocking him onto his back. His spine hit the metal, sending a spasm down his legs.

The cattle grid! Why hadn't he thought of that before? A weapon hidden under the surface. Clayton looked through the gaps in the cattle grid.

Shielding his eyes from the dust, Clayton plunged his hand into a gap. Spindly strands of what he assumed – what he hoped – were spider webs wrapped around his fingers as he prodded the bottom. Amid the dirt, his fingertips touched something solid.

Sand and straw lashed against the back of his neck as he reached down further and clasped the object. Expectations weighing heavy on his chest, he drew his arm free.

A stick? Fat lot of use that is. He glanced up hoping Rusty had returned, but all he saw was the Red King. He turned. The sheds were near. He could make a run for it. Once in the shed, he'd have some shelter, but Rusty was still out there.

He held the long stick aloft and thrust it towards the Red King.

The demon's chuckle filled the air. "It won't work for long." Its mouth opened as it laughed and through its mouth sunlight filtered through the haze.

"What won't work –" Before Clayton finished speaking, the end of the stick shimmered silver in the sun. For the first time he actually *looked* at the stick. The end was tapered and glistened like marble, just like the tip of a spear. The realisation gave him a burst of confidence. He brought the spear back over his shoulder and hurled it at the demon, using the Red King's mouth as a bullseye for aim.

The weapon struck below his chin, cutting out the cackling laugh.

A puff of dust that was once his head dissipated into the air. The rest of the body scattered in the breeze until it became indistinguishable from the surrounding haze.

Clayton exhaled a breath he didn't know he was holding. He peered towards the horizon, hoping Rusty was still there.

"Rusty!"

Barking echoed across the paddock and a tiny dot of fur bounded towards him. As she ran closer, Clayton realised Rusty was clutching the spear in her mouth.

Clayton staggered through the dusty haze that used to be the Red King as she galloped towards him as if they were playing and dropped the spear at his feet.

It was all too easy. Even Waringa had been doubtful that the weapon would work. Clayton looked to the sky, hopeful of some sign of the rain spirit, but besides the lingering haze and the burning sun there was nothing.

Rusty looked up at Clayton with pleading eyes and barked.

"I'm not playing, girl."

Something still didn't feel right. A dense static prickled his skin and the heat of the air burned his throat and skin more than it should have.

Rusty barked, picked up the spear and dropped it again.

"Cut it out. I'm not playing," he said to her. Clayton hobbled across the paddock and grabbed his shoe.

Rusty picked up the spear again and galloped off into the haze.

"I'm not chasing you," Clayton called. His swollen ankle throbbed as he pulled on his shoe. "Rusty, I'm going back now," he called out across the paddock, but she didn't respond.

The dust was still thick and harsh in the back of his throat, and he covered his nose and mouth with the bottom of his t-shirt. Wind skirted around his legs, wafting small spirals of dust into the air. To his left, a small willy-willy darted across the paddock, picking up strands of straw.

Something reverberated through the ground. Alongside him, the willy-willy changed shape and ploughed towards him, churning up soil. There were no arms this time. It looked like a vertical slug, a thick tail of dust trailed behind its body.

"I am afraid that weapon was hidden for a reason," the demon's hollow voice boomed through the air. "It was mine. Hidden by me. Reserved for a time when it was needed most. It is wood, fuel for the fire."

What fire? Confused, Clayton started for the shed at a run.

"Do you believe I have been cruel up 'til this point? I can scorch the land. If you think the land is parched now and the stock are starving, wait and see."

Clayton stopped in the shed doorway and turned. "No! You can't make it any worse for Dad. We need rain. I'll find another weapon. One that will turn you to mud." His voice carried in the wind and echoed in the shed behind him.

"Weapon?" The creature crossed the cattle grid and kept coming as it spoke. "No weapon will defeat me. You have added more fuel to the fire."

Again with the fire reference. Across the paddocks, there was dust but no sign of smoke.

The creature grew until it towered over him.

Clayton backed away, keeping his eyes fixed on the demon.

The Red King drew in its slug-like tail then flicked it forward, hurling stones into the air. The stones sparked as they struck the earth, and a lone rank tussock of grass blazed.

If he wasn't so scared, Clayton might have laughed. "You've killed most of the grass on the paddocks. There's nothing to burn."

The Red King's cheeks expanded as if it were going to explode.

Perhaps the weapon actually worked.

But the spirit didn't explode, it blew. The gust of wind from its mouth billowed Clayton's t-shirt against his body, his fringe whipped into his eyes and a roaring noise made him turn. The burning tussock grew into a slug-shaped flame as tall as an emu. The spindly flame darted across the ground on a thin tail and then divided into two flames, then four, then eight. The fiery slug-like bodies danced along the ground and towards the shed. Towards his dad's stock feed and bales.

Clayton ran. Pain seared through his ankle. He pushed on. So did the fiery creatures. They jumped from saltbush to saltbush, singed every blade of grass between the Red King and the shed and crackled with flame.

The fiery bodies thronged around the tin shed, tails licking the earth.

There was no water nearby. How was he going to put it out? He darted past the fire, into the shed and searched for anything to fight the blaze outside. A hessian sack of grain rested against the back wall behind the header. Clayton raced to the workbench, found a razor and slashed open the top of the sack. He felt light-headed as he looked at the grain. Dad was going to go bananas.

Crackling resonated behind him. Taking a breath, hoping his dad would forgive him, Clayton emptied the grain on the ground. He ran outside the shed and beat the flaming creatures with the sack. The hairs of his legs singed and his ankle throbbed, but he whacked the ground over and over until the grass smouldered in defeat.

A gust of wind belted his ankles. The grass glowed bright orange with renewed vigour.

The Red King towered behind him. The demon puffed, driving the flame into the shed. Clayton tried to beat the flame as it ran across the ground, but it moved quicker than he could. Gathering momentum and energy, it ignited hay scattered on the ground, skirting around the towering pile of bales.

"Stop!" cried Clayton. "You can't do this to Dad." He pummelled the sack on the flames as they licked the edges of the haystack.

The Red King suddenly slunk into the earth like water funnelling down a drainpipe. For a second, Clayton thought the Red King would let him be, but the earth trembled under his feet and the hay bales shook.

Black smoke emerged from the top of the haystack, making its way towards the roof of the shed.

"I can do far worse to your dad." The response came from the stream of smoke billowing out of the hay bales.

Clayton backed away. "Who are you?"

"I am smoke. I am heat." The familiar hollow cackling voice resonated in Clayton's chest. "I am dust. I can be a dry hot wind. I can destroy all." The smoke condensed, forming a slender body and thick limbs.

How could it be him? The demon had vanished into the earth.

"You seem confused, boy."

"Who . . . who are you?" asked Clayton, although he didn't really want to hear the answer. "You're not the Red King. You can't be."

"Really?"

"You're not red," Clayton said, trying to convince himself more than anything. The Red King was meant to be red.

"Is that so?" The smoky creature glowed like a ruby as the bales burst into flames. "Red enough for you?"

The temperature radiating from the blaze burned Clayton's face. He held the sack out in front of him, trying to shield himself against the raging heat.

"Stop! That's Dad's feed. He'll hate me." Clayton tried to approach the blazing tower of hay, but the heat forced him away.

In his smoky form, the Red King crept along the ceiling. Then it divided, streaming in opposite directions like bullhorns until it split again into separate smoky creatures. They grew. On one side of the shed, smoke lashed his dad's workbench, at the other end smoke poured across Davo's tractor.

Darker whiffs of smoke formed facial features on the two creatures. They laughed in unison. Fire burst from their open mouths, smothering the farm equipment in flames.

Clayton glanced between Dad's tools, the stock feed, and Davo's tractor, and rushed to his brother's vehicle. The Red King licked the bonnet and roof. The remaining green and gold paint blistered and blackened.

Clayton beat the flames, but the smoke made his eyes water and the scene blur. He tried to swish away the smoke with the sack, but as he did so the creature divided in half. The more he swished the Red King away the more it separated. The fragments of smoke and flame grew and soon the Red King was in a dozen sections, lingering above, in front, behind, all-around Clayton. All of the versions sniggering.

Smoky tendrils clasped at Clayton's throat. He ducked, covering his eyes, but the smoke poured through his mouth and nostrils and into his lungs.

A loud bang echoed throughout the shed as the tractor tyres blew. Coughing, and with eyes stinging and head spinning, Clayton ducked low and crawled. The smoke became so thick he couldn't see the way out. He kept crawling, hoping to hit the side of the shed and feel his way out, but all he collided with were stray tools that scorched his knees and hands as he pushed them out of the way.

The smoky creatures billowed around him, enveloped him, and clasped him in their wispy appendages. Clayton covered his mouth with his t-shirt, but the Red King penetrated the fabric.

Amber eyes blazed through the smoke.

"Waringa?"

Clayton thought he heard the fox calling back with a hollow bark. Above the amber eyes, a red eye winked. And then a blue. Red eye, blue eye, red eye. They kept winking at him, and Waringa's bark turned to a long wailing cry like an alarm or a siren.

"Waringa, help." Clayton barely heard his own hoarse voice.

Something grasped the collar of his t-shirt and pulled, dragging his body against the hard ground and grazing his legs. He tried to open his eyes but the smoke stung, his eyes watered, the scene blurred. And faded.

CHAPTER 7

In the dark, a fly buzzed faintly in Clayton's ear. He strained to hear it. Now it didn't sound like a fly, but the rumbling and whirring of Davo's tractor. Clayton listened to the soothing melody. He must be on the tractor with Davo, but he could tell through closed eyelids that it was dark. Was Davo fallowing the paddock at night? Of course he was. The headlights peered into the gloom. Davo sat in the driver's seat, Akubra perched on his head and sunnies perched on top of his hat despite it being night.

"You know what Nudge says, 'work her and she'll come'." Davo turned the tractor around in a wide circle as he reached the fence line. "Not entirely sure about his philosophy though," he whispered. Davo tilted his Akubra up and peered at Clayton with large dark eyes, like Dad's. "Wanna drive?"

Sure. Clayton didn't hear his voice. Had he actually spoken? He tried to shuffle over on the seat but couldn't move.

The grumbling of the tractor conked out; and in the distance, Clayton heard yelling. Screaming.

Probably Dad yelling at me for not doing the dishes. Keep driving, said Clayton although his throat felt so raw the words didn't seem to surface. *Tractor's sounding a bit sick, Davo.*

"Yeah, she ain't too happy these days. This was Dad's old beast. Need to buy a new one." Davo was suddenly standing out in the paddock with his back to Clayton and the tractor. "Hardly seems worth it though."

What doesn't? Clayton strained to get up from the tractor but something was stopping him.

"Buying a new tractor. Working the paddock." Davo's voice drifted off. "Any of it. Why bother?"

Someone was shouting again from across the paddock. ". . . he was just lying there. Oh, God. He's not moving."

Lots of people shouting, "Get him inside!"

The shouting subsided and Davo was standing in his kitchen with his back still to Clayton. The kelpie puppy scurried around Davo's feet, trying to lick his legs.

I can cook you a steak, said Clayton. *Mum was showing me how to make it so it isn't overcooked.*

"I ain't hungry, buddy. I'm going to bed. You should go home."

No, I don't want to.

"Go home, Clayton."

The shouting resumed from outside. And a robot was chattering in the distance. A rhythmical whirr . . . click . . . whirr . . . click.

"Come on, sweetie. Open your eyes."

Since when did his brother use words like sweetie? The confusion subsided. It wasn't night-time anymore; his eyes were just closed. He didn't want to open them. He shut them tighter and concentrated. Davo was inside, Akubra still perched on his head even though they were indoors.

The voices were louder.

"He's only mucking around as he misses Da – him." It was a feminine voice, certainly not Davo's. "Maybe we should discuss it with –"

"Shut it!"

"I didn't mean . . . it's just that you're not coping, Walt. You're both not –"

"I'm coping. I just don't give a bleeding shit. He left us! Do you expect me to give a shit after what he bloody well did?"

"Walt, don't use that language in front of him."

"He ain't even awake."

Clayton shut his eyes even tighter and tried not to focus on his dad's words. Surrounded by his parents' arguing, he heard a machine whirring nearby and felt something wrapped around his ears and under his nose. Reluctantly, Clayton flicked his eyes open and pulled at a tube around his head. He realised he was in an unfamiliar bed with medical equipment around him. And Davo wasn't here. Davo was never going to be here again. Clayton's eyes watered. He tried to swallow the lump in his throat, but the more he tried to stop crying the faster the tears rolled down his cheeks.

"Hey, sweetie. Leave the tube there." Mum smiled, though her eyes were red and puffy with tears.

Clayton lifted his hand to wipe away his tears, only to find a needle in his wrist and pulse monitor on his finger.

"Don't worry about that," Mum said. "The smoke's probably making your eyes water."

Dad stood a few feet from the bed, arms crossed over his chest, Akubra tilted forwards so that Clayton couldn't see his eyes.

"Dad," Clayton's voice croaked.

Dad pushed back his hat and glared at Clayton.

"Did it get his tractor?"

"The tractor?" There was an edge to Dad's voice. "You're worried about that bloody heck . . . You . . . you." His dad studied the medical instruments at the side of the bed, but he didn't seem interested in them.

Look at me, Dad. Clayton tried to catch his eye, but Dad refused to look in his direction.

"Dad?"

"Don't flipping talk to me right now."

Tears welled up again and Clayton shut his eyes so Dad couldn't see how weak he was.

Footsteps echoed from around the corner and a doctor popped his head into the ward. "Not interrupting, am I?"

"No." Mum said. "Are the results back?"

"Chest X-rays and blood chem are clear and there's no evidence of any damage to the tissues in the respiratory system. Even his throat looks relatively unscathed. Just a few superficial burns and scratches and heat exhaustion."

"Really?" Dad asked.

There was no smile, no discernible emotion, and he still wouldn't look at him, but was there a hint of relief in his dad's voice?

"There was smoke everywhere," Dad said.

Smoke? It was the Red King that got me. Clayton knew he couldn't explain that to his dad, though.

"It's amazing, but he's fine." The doctor bent down and rubbed the top of Clayton's head. "You were very lucky. I think you can even go home." He removed the drip from Clayton's hand and pressed a wad of gauze against the needle site. "Press on this."

"Yeah," his dad began, as if reassuring himself. "Yeah, of course, he's okay. He's a Hopper. He ain't weak." Dad turned to him and glared. "Just stupid."

Clayton closed his eyes to shut out the disappointment in his dad's gaze. He tried to imagine Davo's farm again, but he couldn't picture his brother and he couldn't block out the background chatter of his parents and the doctor telling him to take things easy. How was he supposed to take it easy?

"Any signs of fever, nausea, vomiting or anything unusual then come back in. Otherwise I'll drop by tomorrow arvo." The doctor removed the gauze from Clayton's hand and replaced it with a plaster. "I'd say you can have a few days off school too." The doctor beamed a broad, patronising grin.

Clayton had forgotten school holidays were ending. He was in no hurry to return to school and put up with the horrendously long bus trip. Besides, he needed those extra few days to find Waringa.

"No working on the paddock either," the doctor said. "You can take off the nasal cannula." He pointed to the tube around Clayton's head. "And I'll get a wheelchair and your discharge papers."

"He don't need a wheelchair," Dad said. "He's a farmer. Only wheels he needs are a ute and tractor. Right, Clay?"

Clayton didn't want to argue, but his head felt fuzzy and his calves were cramping.

The doctor smiled. "I'll get a wheelchair. Clayton, you have to take it easy for a few days, okay?"

Dad didn't speak on the way out of the hospital or during the long drive back to Paddle Creek Station, and Mum resumed her idle chitchat about the weather and what they should cook for dinner. Dad didn't even raise an eyebrow as they drove past Reggie's paddock where the topsoil had dried and drifted against the boundary fence and partly across the road.

At his mum's insistence, Clayton rested before tea. He nestled down with a book, but inside were no faraway lands, enchanted forests or mythical creatures. It was filled with ordinary words on the page. Fatigue quickly took hold and he drifted off.

When Mum called him for dinner it felt like only seconds later, but outside the window, it was already growing dark.

Clayton felt giddy as he sat up, his energy drained away, and the room felt stuffy and claustrophobic. Something was different. Except for Mum calling his name again, it was quiet. That wasn't anything new – his dad rarely spoke these days – still, something wasn't right. Something niggled at him.

He walked into the lounge room and heard his parents muttering from the kitchen.

"Don't be daft. The bales had only been there for a few days, hardly long enough to self-combust." Clayton could tell his dad was still angry. The tiniest part of Clayton was happy that he showed some emotion, but mostly it hit Clayton in his guts, making him feel helpless.

"I'm just saying it might not have been . . ." Mum's voice drifted off, and she appeared in the doorway of the living room. "Hey, sweetie. Thought I heard you. How are you feeling?"

"Fine." Clayton walked towards the kitchen but hesitated when he saw his dad slumped over the laptop at the kitchen table. Dad didn't look up or even acknowledge his presence.

"I've made roast beef and I've put in plenty of turnip and parsnip for you. The doctor said your throat looks fine, but if anything hurts, or if your stomach isn't up to it, I can make something else."

"Will you stop flapping those lips, woman," Dad said, still hunched in his chair. "Do you have any idea what you've done?"

Clayton struggled to work out what his mum could've done to upset Dad, before he realised he was directing the sudden outburst at him.

"We had the entire fire brigade trying to put out the flames. They reckon it's going to be smouldering for days. I have no feed left. The shed is irreparable. Do you have any idea how much that all cost?"

Clayton tried to block out the tirade. *I'm trying to bring rain and make it better*, he thought.

"Oi! You listening? I'm talking thousands of dollars. Did you hear that? And I ain't even considering what tools I've lost in the shed. And how did you manage to lose your Akubra?"

"Walt. It'll be okay," Mum chipped in, but Dad just ignored her.

"How do you expect us to feed the stock now? Have you seen the sheep's muscles? They're concave. You frickin' spilled all my grain too."

"There's feed further north," said Clayton. Going to Davo's property would do his dad good, but he knew the comment was useless. It was going to take more than starving stock to get Dad onto Davo's land.

Dad ignored him.

"Clayton," Mum whispered, shaking her head.

Tell him, Mum. Tell Dad he should graze Davo's land. Tell him Davo's property still exists – his memory still exists.

"Seriously, Clayton. It was one simple task."

The phone rang, cutting Dad off. He grabbed it before anyone else could get there.

Clayton looked to Mum for support, but she was gazing intently at Dad with concern.

Something still didn't seem right. Despite his parents' shouting and arguing, the house seemed quieter than normal.

"Take a seat," Mum said, pointing at a towering plate of food on the table.

Clayton sat and nibbled at the roast vegetables until his hunger got the better of him and he gobbled them down.

"Take it easy, sweetie." She placed a huge glass of water in front of him.

"Thanks," he said, but Mum wasn't looking at him. Her eyes were still focused on Dad.

"Yeah, I understand, Nick," Dad said down the phone.

Nick. Where had Clayton heard that name? Certainly none of the local farmers or farmhands were called Nick.

"We still need to discuss whether we can get the cash together. I'll get back to you tomorrow arvo. Cheers, mate." He put down the receiver.

As the receiver clicked, so did the name in Clayton's mind. Nick. The person Dad got to vaccinate the stock. Nick. The person Dad got to come out to help Davo when he had a cow suffering a breech birth.

"No!" Clayton stood and looked around frantically. She hadn't been asleep at the foot of his bed; she wasn't loping around the lounge room in her naive manner; she wasn't trying to scavenge food underneath the table. "No." He couldn't manage to say anything else. If he said it, it would ring true.

CHAPTER 8

"**R**usty burned her paws and snout pretty badly, but we'll work something out," Mum said softly.

"Em," Dad began. "We don't have that kind of money to waste –"

"Waste?" blurted Clayton, now realising what Dad was saying. "Of course we can find the money. She's family!"

"She isn't even ours and she ain't the most useful sheepdog we've ever had."

"You can't!" He looked between his mum and dad, waiting for them to tell him they'd do anything to save Rusty. Weakness rippled through his legs. It must have shown, for Mum was at his side, supporting his weight with an arm around his waist.

"We haven't decided yet." She squeezed his waist. "It's just finances are so tight at the moment . . ."

Clayton ripped himself from her embrace and backed away from his parents, shaking his head. They weren't serious. Surely? Rusty was Davo's. The only thing of his left. She was family. They couldn't put her down. Were they punishing him for the fire or punishing Davo for . . . leaving them? It wasn't Davo's fault for leaving or not training Rusty before he died.

"It wasn't his fault Rusty isn't the most obedient dog we've ever had. I can train her better."

Dad turned his back on Clayton, hands on hips. "I ain't talking about this."

"Why don't you care?" Clayton backed away down the corridor. The floor blurred under his feet and he leaned on the wall to steady himself.

"Clay, sweetie. You need to sit down. The doctor said you

have to take it easy."

Somehow, Clayton had made it to the front door.

"Clay, obey your mother and sit down!" Dad yelled, his voice so loud it vibrated through Clayton's bones. "It's just a dog," he continued. "He didn't care about his dog. He left her here. He left you. Why do you care? He didn't care about you."

Why would his dad say that? Davo loved him; he loved Rusty. Clayton leaned heavily on the door handle and when it opened he stumbled outside onto the porch and down the steps.

"Clayton, get back here this instant!"

Dad's bellowing voice trailed off as Clayton started to run. He didn't know where he was running to, or how he found the strength, he only knew he had to get away. Neither Mum or Dad would be able to keep up with him, but once they reached the ute they'd find him in no time and then he'd have no chance of making things right again. If he could only bring the rain back, feed would regenerate, finances would improve and everything, including Rusty, would be okay.

A slender trail of smoke from the shed was visible in the moonlight. Clayton hoped the quad was still north of that.

The shed looked like the letter 'M'. The tin above the bales had collapsed and, in the middle of the shed, the once towering pile of bales had slumped to a charred heap. A bulldozer sat outside along with burned hay that the fire-fighters had obviously raked across the paddock. The damp, smouldering remains wafted a smell like rotten seaweed towards him. Among the rubble and ash, the workbench was still relatively intact. He ran his hand across the wall until he came to the hook that held the torch. The plastic had melted around the rim but other than that, it looked unscathed. He flicked the switch but nothing happened. Mimicking his dad, he hit the end of the torch on his thigh several times and the spotlight shone across the ground.

In the distance, he heard his dad hollering. Clayton darted

from the shed and scanned the fence with the torch, looking for the gap. He orientated himself in the right direction, turned off the torch so his parents wouldn't see the light, and ran towards the cattle grid.

His ankle was aching and his legs burned, but he kept running, needing to escape the reality that awaited him back home. In the dim moonlight, he managed to spot the gap in the fence. He tiptoed across the cattle grid, anxious about getting his foot trapped again, and headed west towards where he'd left the quad.

He flicked the torch back on, probed the circle of light to the west, saw the torch shine upon the metal of the vehicle and turned it off straight away. The ute's headlights weren't behind him. Maybe they weren't following him. Perhaps Dad was so angry he didn't *care* if Clayton ran off. Clayton shut his eyes, trying to dismiss the thought; but when he did, he still saw Dad's disappointed face.

The quad was exactly where he'd left it, with the key still in the ignition. He paused to catch his breath and work out where he was going to go. The answer came swiftly. He hopped into the quad, crossed his fingers and turned the ignition. It started on the first go.

Without turning on either the headlights or torch, Clayton managed to reverse and steer in the right direction. Alone in the dark, the journey seemed to take forever. There was no sign of his parents trailing him. He wasn't sure whether to be relieved or disappointed.

Swerving to dodge the sporadic bushes along the way, the trailer clunked and rattled behind him.

"Please, be quiet," he whispered anxiously to the quad bike.

His parents were still nowhere in sight. Surely, Mum would guess where he would go. He drove along the derelict internal fence line, then detoured across the paddock.

As he drove near, headlights behind him squinted through

the dark. Clayton jumped off quickly when he reached the gate, leaving the quad idling. He unlatched the gate, opened it and, after driving through to Davo's property, shut it again. He wasn't taking any chances of Dad suspecting he'd fled this way.

Clayton drove the quad along the overgrown track, making the trailer rattle as it scaled small saltbushes and clumps of grass. He parked around the rear, crept along the back wall to the corner of the house, and peered back towards the gate.

"Clayton." He heard the anguish in Mum's voice. As the ute's lights grew larger, her voice became louder and the anguish intensified.

Two beams of light streamed big and bright. Clayton stepped away, pressed his back to the wall and tried to quieten his breathing.

"Clayton," Mum cried out. The gate creaked. "Clayton? Please, everything will be okay."

No, it wouldn't. Dad was anything but okay and there was only one thing Clayton could think of to fix that now, but his mum sounded so upset. He wanted so badly to run out and hug her.

Clayton heard the soil crunching as she ran towards the house.

"Clayton, sweetie?"

The timber of the steps and deck around Davo's house groaned. The door handle rattled as if shaken. There was no sound indicating Dad had bothered to come to the house. Maybe he could run up to her. Now she was near his house, she might even talk about Davo.

"God, he's not here. Where is he? Clayton! Clayton!" There was so much pain in her voice.

The timber of the steps and deck creaked again, and footsteps drew closer. And closer.

"Em, he ain't here." That was Dad's voice, but it sounded

so distant. He still couldn't come onto Davo's property.

The footsteps stopped. "He might be inside."

"We've got the only key. No one's going in there."

"Clayton!"

"Em," Dad's voice intensified. "Let's try the dam." There was a hint of concern in his voice.

For a while, Clayton couldn't hear anything, but then the footsteps crunched back towards the fence and died away. The ute's engine started up, and Clayton stood motionless until the noise faded. He exhaled.

No key. Clayton smiled. So Dad thought.

Footsteps crunched nearby, making Clayton spin. With the moonlight obscured by cloud and the headlights from the ute gone, he couldn't see more than a few metres in front of him. More footsteps. Which direction were they coming from? Had his mum and dad tricked him into coming out? Clayton backed away from the corner, trying to tread lightly on the ground. The footsteps drew closer. His foot hit a solid object and something grasped his shoulder from behind. He spun. A pair of amber eyes gazed at him from above. The clouds parted, revealing Waringa, his fur glistening in the moonlight.

The fox stood taller than before and looked down at Clayton with iridescent eyes. Shining fur replaced the mange at the base of his tail. And he no longer smelled.

"What are you waiting for?" asked Waringa. "You know what you came here for."

"I know," said Clayton. He walked around to the front of the building and stared at the heavy wooden front door. "I want to, but . . ." Why did it frighten his so much? "This serpent might not even know how to defeat the Red King. Who's to say it isn't an ally of the Red King?"

"Maybe it is. But it could hold the solution."

"Dad will never forgive me for going in there. He hates me as it is."

"Time is not on your side. Nor your dad's. And certainly

not Rusty's."

Waringa's eyes bored into Clayton's soul. "Sometimes to help those we love we need to hurt them."

Clayton's stomach ached at the thought of angering his dad further. It felt like a willy-willy was spinning out of control in his guts, trying to escape. Despite his apprehension, he knew he had to go in there.

Clayton walked back to the trailer and retrieved the shovel still lying in the back.

"His alliance may be ambiguous, but you do not want to anger this serpent," said Waringa.

"I'm not," said Clayton defiantly. "I'm just protecting myself."

"With a shovel?"

"That's how Dad kills snakes."

"And do you do everything your dad does?" Waringa's tone cut to Clayton's core. "Wear his hat. Eat his food." Waringa padded around the corner and disappeared out of sight.

"Wait!" Clayton raced around the corner to find the yard empty. He flashed the torch across the paddock. "Waringa?"

Clayton wandered to the steps leading up to the front porch and panned the light across the wooden decking.

"Fine, leave me alone!" shouted Clayton. He waited for Waringa to re-emerge from wherever he was hiding. "I'll do this by myself then." Clayton grasped the shovel handle more firmly. "Waringa?" His voice trembled.

Silence engulfed the balmy night air: no footsteps or voices filled the void. Clouds obscured the Moon and stars until the only light was the torch beam glinting upon the spider web spanning the veranda posts.

Everyone left when he needed them most. Clayton wasn't going to desert Rusty. At this point, he would do anything to bring rain.

As Clayton ducked under the orb weaver's web, his

determination wavered. "It's just a house. It's just a house." The mantra did little to reassure him. "I'm being absurd. I've been here hundreds of times when Davo was here," he muttered.

He rested the shovel against the wall. Behind the rickety deck chairs sat the old work boot full of soil and a dried stick that was once a plant. Fibrous roots poked through holes in the toe and heel.

Clayton teased the spider webs from around the boot and plucked the tiny skeleton key from underneath.

Although the plant was brittle now, Davo had revelled in its growth before.

"At least something's growin'. I reckon Rusty's been peeing on it," Davo had said the day he showed Clayton his hiding spot. "If I could get Rusty to take a leak on the crops, I'd be laughing."

"Why can't I tell Dad where the key is?"

"I want to have a go at the farm by myself, so I don't want Dad poking his nose into what I'm doing. I gotta prove to Dad I can do it." There had been a hint of uncertainty in his brother's voice.

I can do this myself too, thought Clayton. He wiped the dirt from the key onto his shorts and slid it into the lock. His fingers strained to turn the key, but it eventually clicked. The sound of the lock sent a shudder down his spine. For a second, he hesitated. There was something about the house and something about opening the house with the key that filled him with fear.

"It's absurd. It's Davo's house," he said to himself. He shoved the door with his shoulder. The hinges groaned in protest but the door swung open.

Clayton flashed the torch into the gloom. All that was visible was dust floating in the beam of light and a pair of work boots sitting in the front hallway. Clayton picked up the shovel and realised how sweaty his palms were. He wiped them on his shorts, gripped the shovel tighter and stepped inside. The front hallway was so quiet. Like how a cloudy night absorbed all light, this house absorbed all sound. He couldn't hear his footsteps or his own breath, even though his chest heaved raggedly.

Clayton shuffled along the hallway, pressing his back against the wall, keeping an eye out for any sign of movement. The air tasted dry and musty and overcame his senses, but he continued towards the lounge.

He scanned the room. The torchlight fell on the couch. Its upholstery slightly worn, the white fabric tarnished with oil and grease and dirt. A pair of workpants still lay draped over an armchair and worn socks dotted the floor. Behind the couch, the torch shone upon an engine. Spanners and a can of WD40 surrounded the machinery. No one had packed up any of Davo's things. The scene filled Clayton with dread, but he wasn't sure why.

There was no serpent. There was nothing here, nothing but oppressive air and silence. The kitchen was no different: old coffee cup on the bench, paperwork scattered on the kitchen table, a bag of fertiliser on a chair.

Clayton rested the shovel against the chair and put the torch down on the table, letting it shine on the paperwork. He sifted through a pile of bills, tractor and shed catalogues, and a note written on the back of an envelope that simply said 'Sorry'.

His chest tightened. He had a distinct feeling of déjà vu that he'd come across all this before, exactly as it was now. His head hurt as he strained to recollect why it looked so familiar.

Rustling echoed behind him. Or was it from below? Clayton grasped the shovel and held it aloft.

"Waringa?" asked Clayton hopefully.

With his free hand, Clayton snatched the torch and shone it in the direction of the noise. Hissing like a mad cat resonated from behind the wooden door that led to the garage.

CHAPTER 9

Clayton imagined Waringa's persistent voice in his head telling him to keep going.

"It might just be a feral cat," Clayton said to no one in particular. He struggled to hold the torch steady, and the circle of light bounced around on the door. Then it slowly decreased in diameter as the torch dimmed.

"Don't die on me now." Clayton slapped the torch against his thigh and the light brightened.

Hesitantly, he shuffled towards the door. The warped timber jammed on the threshold and wouldn't budge as he pushed it. He rammed his shoulder against the door. It gave way and he stumbled forward, dropping the torch. The light vanished as the torch clanked down a couple of steps.

The contents of his stomach curdled in fear as he was plunged into darkness. Acidic bile surged up his throat and he grasped the handrail of the stairs and leaned on the shovel with his other hand to steady himself. He took a deep breath and swallowed, forcing the bile back down.

Clayton clasped the shovel tighter and tapped his foot in front of him, finding his way down the stairs in the dark.

His foot landed on something round, his ankle rolled, the shovel fell from his hands and Clayton tumbled onto the concrete floor of the garage. The same ankle he'd hurt before twinged. Blood pulsated near the joint. He pointed and flexed his foot, clasping it in both hands.

Something rustled above him. Along the walls and floor, there was the sound of slithering. Clayton felt the concrete floor around him, desperately searching for the shovel.

The slithering resonated along the ground. Something metal tolled and clanked on the concrete. Clayton felt for the handle of the shovel and grasped it with two hands.

"Ssstay your blade, mortal." The drawn-out voice echoed throughout the garage, growing nearer. "What busssiness have you here?"

"The Red King." Clayton's voice caught in his throat. "I have to defeat him."

"You wake me from my ssslumber for ansssswers you already posssesss."

"What!" Clayton clambered to his feet and held the shovel forward. "If I knew, don't you think I would've have gotten rid of him by now?"

"Deep inssside, you know the magic that isss needed."

"Magic? What, like spells? I don't know any."

"Of coursssse you do. Ssspells are but wordsss. Wordss with power." The voice was almost beneath his feet now.

"Get back!" Clayton staggered backwards and swung the shovel forward. "What spells? What words?"

"Do not thrussst that blade at me."

Something smooth and silky brushed against Clayton's leg. Clayton swiped the shovel haphazardly in the dark, losing his balance and all sense of orientation.

"Get away," he whispered.

"Do I sscare you? Ssssuch weaknesss," the voice sang out behind him. "Your father would not approve." The serpent's voice spoke above him now. It sounded as if it were sliding over wood. Around wood. Along the rafters on the ceiling.

Clayton looked up, but there wasn't a hint of moonlight filtering into the garage. Would the serpent strike from above? Clayton shuddered at the possibility. The shovel slipped in his sweaty palms. The slithering noise ceased. In the ensuing silence, Clayton heard his heart pounding in his chest.

"Your fear sssshows. Faccce it. You are meant to plough sssoil, not defeat that which liesss within it."

The creature was on the move. Down the walls. *I have to stay brave for Dad and Rusty*, thought Clayton. The serpent glided along the floor. Clayton brought the shovel down hard. It clanged against the concrete.

"Ssstop," the serpent screeched in a shrill voice to Clayton's left.

He whacked the ground again. This time, the shovel hit something soft, and a drawn-out mew echoed around the garage. The creature was still on the move, working its way to higher ground. Clayton tried to follow the sound, but his head kept spinning. Whether it was the dark or after-affects from the smoke, Clayton didn't know. All he knew was he had to work out what magic he needed to defeat the Red King, and he was getting nowhere dodging this temperamental beast.

Clayton stretched his free arm in front of him, looking for the wall, a bench, the stairs or anything to orientate himself, but his hands found nothing to hold. Instead, his toe collided with a hard surface. The jolt made him drop the shovel and sent a dull throb through the ankle he'd sprained. Clayton bent down and ran his fingers over the surface in front of him. The stairs. He'd rolled his ankle on the torch on the stairs. Clayton squatted and felt for the torch.

The slithering noise resumed above him. Clayton moved further from the stairs, patting the ground desperately.

"You will sssuffer for taking a ssswing at me."

"Yeah?" Clayton's hand fell upon the torch and he fumbled for the switch. "You're just a slithering snake. What you going to do?" The tiniest ray of light shone from the torch.

"Cassst away your lightssss. I musssst remain in the darknessss. You ssshall not ssssee me. You cannot!"

Clayton panned the torch upwards. The ring of light barely made an impression on the wooden beam above.

"Turn off the light or I ssshall hurt you. I will hit you where it hurtsss mossssst." The serpent spat the words with spite and fury, but Clayton still couldn't see it.

Clayton swallowed hard. "Come on," he begged, hitting the torch on his thigh.

For a split second, the light shone brightly and he saw it. The serpent's tail curled over the rafter, its neck bent into a loop. Pain soared through Clayton's body, tingled his skin, pierced his skull. He averted his eyes. Why did it hurt so much? Was it like a Basilisk where he wasn't meant to look at it? The torch beam faded to a pinprick of light. Something slippery brushed against his arm, knocking the torch from his grasp. The serpent bombarded him from above, hitting his torso and head and making his body ache.

Flailing his arms above his head, Clayton tried to fend off the serpent, but the onslaught was unrelenting. He reached for the torch and shone it into the room. In the dim light, he just made out the shovel. Clayton covered his head with his free arm and clambered along the ground, grasped the shovel in one hand and got shakily to his feet. He swung and the shovel collided with something tall, which grunted. He shone the light up to see Waringa standing there nursing his paw.

"Your aim is lousy." Waringa rubbed his paw.

Clayton staggered to his feet with the shovel poised to strike. He scanned the room. "Where did it go?"

"It fled. Why did you injure it?"

"It was hurting me."

"Hurting how?"

Clayton had no words to describe the pain he was feeling. Something ached deep inside, like venom was running through his veins. "That's not the point. Where were you?"

"I'm here now. I'm here when you need me."

"Need?" scoffed Clayton. "Fat lot of good you've done. Dad's angry with me. The serpent didn't tell me what spell I needed to free the rain spirits. Now it's angry at me too. It said it'd hurt –"

Hit me where it hurts most. The words finally resonated within Clayton and dread surfaced from the pit of his stomach.

"You said it fled. Fled which way?" Clayton shone the torch directly in Waringa's face but got little in the way of a response.

Waringa raised his snout and sniffed the air.

"Hurry up! Where did it go?" Clayton didn't bother waiting for a response. Deep down, he knew where the serpent could hurt him most.

CHAPTER 10

Clayton ran up the stairs and out the front door. He didn't bother waiting for Waringa and didn't stop to close the door either. Back at the quad, he threw the shovel and failing torch into the trailer and started the ignition. The engine spat at him with a grunt.

"No, no, no, don't do this to me now. I have to get home." He turned the ignition again, revving the accelerator. The engine turned over reluctantly and he drove around the house and back towards the gate.

"I didn't mean to hurt you. Please, don't hurt them," Clayton begged, even though he knew the serpent couldn't hear. Why had he let his fear show to the serpent? Dad always prided himself on being tough and fearless. Why couldn't Clayton have been like him?

His parents had closed the gate between the two properties. Clayton jumped off before the quad came to a complete standstill and went to unhook the latch.

A heavy-duty padlock was looped around the latch.

"Why?" Clayton tugged on the padlock, realising his dad had shut him in. Why would he do that? Then it hit Clayton, Dad wasn't shutting him in. He'd thought Clayton was elsewhere. He was shutting him out, so he could never go near Davo's place again. Right now, the realisation seemed inconsequential. There was an angry serpent ready to strike his parents.

Clayton shook the gate in desperation. "Please, open. Please, please, please."

An idea struck. He grabbed the shovel from the trailer, brought it over his head and swung it down on the lock like he was chopping wood.

It jarred his elbows and ricocheted off the metal, sending tiny sparks flying into the night air. He hit the lock again and again, only to make the tiniest indent in the metal.

He gazed up in the direction of their house, not that he could even see the lights from here. It'd take hours to walk back, an hour even to run back home.

Giving up on the padlock, he smashed the chain with the spade. The chain didn't snap, but the wood holding the fastening latch split. Dad was always saying the old wooden post needed replacing. He said the posts were more weathered than a rotting tree stump and little good for anything but a place for white snails to rest.

Clayton climbed the gate and straddled his legs over the top so he could bring the shovel down vertical. He aimed for the point where the latch fastened onto the wood and stabbed it hard. The latch tore away from the post and the gate swung open, Clayton still straddling it. He grabbed the gate to steady himself, and after it came to a standstill, he jumped down, got back on the quad and raced along the track.

Now Dad had more fixing to do, but it hardly mattered. Nothing mattered. He doubted his dad could get any angrier with him.

With the quad's headlights guiding the way, he swerved around brittle bushes and rank grass. Twigs crackled under the wheels and saltbushes brushed against his legs as he cut corners of the track.

Soon, his house was a tiny speck on the horizon, silhouetted against the slate grey of the predawn sky. Realising he must've spent ages trying to get through the padlocked gate, he didn't slow down over the next cattle grid just north of the shed. As the quad jolted over the grates it stalled and came to an abrupt halt. Steam sizzled from the bonnet.

"No!" yelled Clayton. He turned the key in the ignition, but the motor gasped and stuttered. Clayton jumped from the quad, grabbed the shovel and bolted towards the house.

For a second, he couldn't see anything unusual, but then he heard rustling in the veggie patch and saw a long dark shape slithering under the Hills Hoist and up the front steps.

"Stop!" He ran faster. His legs burned and his chest tightened. "Stop!" Clayton raced across the garden and over his mum's veggies. Just before the steps, he tripped and fell forward, landing on his knees on the hard dirt.

The serpent struck the front door with so much ferocity that the windows rattled.

"Don't hurt them!"

The serpent turned and stared into Clayton's soul. "Thisss isss not your battle."

The serpent reared up on its tail and lashed out with lightning speed at the door.

Clayton got to his feet and stepped forward, brandishing the shovel. It shook in his hands and the firmer Clayton held it the worse it quivered.

"You cannot ssstop me now." The serpent laughed with a high-pitched hiss.

Clayton lunged forward and brought the tip of the shovel down. It clanked against the steps, missing his target. Before he knew what was happening, the serpent struck Clayton's legs; he fell, and the shovel flew out of reach. He crawled forward and grasped the beast around its middle. Its muscular body squirmed, and its smooth skin slid and rippled through his fingers, forcing his grip to loosen. A tail flicked around his wrist; the serpent's body twisted along his forearm and bicep. The serpent's muscles contracted tighter and tighter. Clayton thrashed it against the step, but the serpent merely hissed and spiralled towards his neck.

"You have lossst." Its tongue flicked in his ear, wet and sandpapery. "Go back to your booksss. You cannot win." The serpent wrapped around his neck, squeezing air from his windpipe.

Dizzy, he tugged at the serpent with his hands. His vision blurring.

"Clay, is that you?" his mum called from inside.

"Mum? Dad?" Clayton mouthed words in the direction of the front door, but no noise came out.

"Sssun!" the serpent spat.

Warm rays beat on the back of Clayton's neck as the sun peered over the horizon and the serpent eased its grip.

Clayton staggered to his feet and rammed his shoulder and arm against the front door, squishing the serpent beneath his body. It hissed. Clayton rammed the door again and the serpent's grip loosened. The creature exhaled like a leaking balloon. It unravelled its tail from his arm and fell on the front porch with a dull thud.

"Clay!" His parent's voices were louder.

Clayton squinted, trying to focus. The serpent lay motionless and limp on the front doorstep.

"No, no, no. No!" Clayton pleaded. "I only wanted to stop you, not hurt you. Get up."

The serpent didn't respond.

"Tell me what magic to use." Clayton reached out and touched the serpent.

"Get up." Its smooth skin shrivelled in the early morning heat, its muscular body shrank. Clayton ran his fingers along the creature. It didn't flinch and the rough surface grazed his fingertips. It came into focus. The creature's neck was coiled into a loop and its body was long and frayed. Its skin turned from metallic green to tan.

"It's the heat burning you up," whispered Clayton. "You were real."

Clayton's heart pounded as the creature continued to wither and contract into nothing more than rope. A rope with a loop. "No." He touched the limp rope tentatively. "What are you doing? Change back! You were real. I saw you. You were moving on the rafters. You are real. Get up!"

Clayton stood shakily. Bile rose up his throat, but he swallowed it back down.

Footsteps thumped along the hallway, coming closer. Clayton took a step back. "Waringa? Where are you?" he whispered.

"Clay, is that you?" From the other side of the door, his mum's voice sounded anxious.

Clayton bolted across the garden and under the Hills Hoist. There was nowhere to hide amid the endless dusty plains and straggly garden.

The front door's latch clicked.

The burned-out shed glinted silver in the morning light. He could make it if he ran fast enough. He scrambled around the smouldering hay and ducked behind the bulldozer just as the front door opened.

Mum gazed across the farm. *Please, don't look down.* Clayton tried to send his thoughts to her. Maybe he did have magic as she turned to go back inside, but Dad appeared by her side. Their voices weren't audible from here, but she shrugged. Dad's eyes glanced down; his lips moved; Mum turned.

Clayton shut his eyes. "Waringa, where are you?" His throat was so dry he could barely speak.

He glanced back to his parents and instantly regretted it. The dead serpent still lay coiled on the ground as a length of rope. Mum slumped to her knees, cradled the rope and rocked back and forth, sobbing and trembling. For a second, it looked like his dad's rigidly held lip started to quiver, but it may have been an illusion, for Dad just grimaced and his face reddened. Clayton wanted to chisel away at that face until he found his father underneath, but nothing seemed to break that stony glare.

"Clay!" Even from here, Clayton heard and felt his Dad's voice resonating through the earth.

Clayton slunk down and ducked his head. He couldn't look at his mum sobbing anymore. He couldn't look at the rope.

"Change back to a serpent! You aren't real." It's not *really* there. He fell to his knees, pain searing through every cell in his body. He shut his eyes, trying to block out the image of the looped rope, but it didn't work. Even with his eyes shut, he could see it, hanging from the rafters. How had he forgotten that?

The memory was still vague. Everything else remained a blur. Everything except Davo. Hanging there.

For months and months before his death, Davo kept insisting he'd been too busy to come over to their place. Eventually, Davo stopped calling. Davo said Clayton could take the quad and come over whenever he wanted. He said if he wasn't home to pinch the key under the boot and come on in. Davo had promised. He promised he'd always be there.

"Clayton!" Dad's bellowing snapped Clayton back to his senses. He wiped tears from his cheeks. Davo had deserted him. Mum was a mess and his dad . . . his dad – nothing could make this right!

Keeping his eye on his parents, Clayton shuffled back towards the shed. The hay still smouldered and stank, but Clayton didn't care. He climbed the blackened metal steps into Davo's tractor. The glass on the driver's side door had shattered. The brittle vinyl had melted in the fire. It dug into his legs as he snuggled into the driver's seat, but he was too exhausted to care. He was too exhausted to care whether the bales would reignite in the heat of the day. And if they did, he'd just let his tears dampen the flames.

CHAPTER 11

Something tapped on the front window. Clayton looked up from the driver's seat. Raindrops fell on the glass, clinging to the surface like mini crystal balls. "It's raining!" he exclaimed.

"That ain't rain." Davo crouched next him.

Clayton rubbed his eyes. The burned, charred tractor was sitting in the shed a second ago. Now he was out on the northern paddock with the grain hopper hooked on the back.

"But it'll pour soon. You'll see," said Davo.

Rain tinkled onto the windscreen sporadically. Against the blackening skies, galahs darted through the air like dodgem cars.

"Throw her into gear," said Davo, pointing to the lever to Clayton's right.

Clayton looked at his brother for a moment, finding his bearings. "I can't reach the pedals."

"That's what the cushion's for, buddy. Help prop you forward."

Clayton squished the cushion behind his back. "Should we really be sowing now?" he asked. "Dad reckons it's still too dry."

"She'll be right. This is the year the drought'll break." Davo gazed out the window as the rain started to ease. "And then everything will be okay," he whispered.

Tap, tap. The rain had stopped but Clayton still heard the water pinging on the glass.

"Everything is going to be okay."

Clayton's eyes flicked open. As he awoke and focused on the shed around him, he saw Waringa tapping on the side of the tractor.

Waringa must be standing on the top step, as he peered directly into Clayton's eyes. He tapped again.

"What do you want?" demanded Clayton. "You deserted me." He looked away from Waringa and out of the shed. The sun had passed the zenith and crept into the western sky. Clayton's neck was aching, and he had an imprint of a lever on his forearm where he'd leaned against it.

Waringa tapped with more determination.

"Will you stop that!" Clayton opened the door. "My head's throbbing." He rubbed his eyes, smearing away dried sleep. Tears welled up in his eyes again, making his headache worse.

"You need to face him head-on," said Waringa.

"Dad can't see me like this. He'd only think I'm weak."

"Not him, the Red King," said Waringa. "You must find the spell and free the rain spirits."

Clayton curled back up in the seat, tucking his legs up to his chest, tears leaking from his eyes. "I can't."

Waringa walked away from the tractor and Clayton realised he hadn't been standing on the step. Waringa had grown again. His fur glistened a brilliant red in the afternoon sunlight.

"You need the rain to return to help Rusty. If your dad gets a good season, things won't be so tight. He'll be happy again. He keeps saying that if it rains it'll be okay." Waringa stood in the sunlight and gazed upwards. "You can't desert them now."

Clayton swallowed a lump cloying in the back of his throat, and rubbed the tears away. Unsteady on his feet, he climbed down to the ground.

"How do I even know that the rain will return if I defeat the Red King?" he asked, following Waringa out of the shed.

Waringa stretched a paw towards the ground. "The rain spirits *want* to return. They just need a helping hand."

Clayton peered at the ring of hills in the distance: dry and brown. "I don't believe you."

The fox waved his hand across the dry plain.

Vibrations shuddered through Clayton's feet and legs. Water spread under his feet; it soaked the dirt, filled the cracks in the clay-pans and tousled twigs and pebbles. In the cracked clay, a tiny green blade of grass germinated before his eyes. It grew and wrapped around his ankle. Creaking resonated through the earth. Clayton looked up. There were fields of wheat, not paddocks but fields. In the sunlight, the wheat shimmered. In the adjacent paddock, a green carpet flourished. Within seconds, it bronzed-off. The breeze caught the seed heads and the paddock waved like a russet ocean. The swell washed towards the hills, which bloomed with the grey and blue of eucalypts. Crowned with fresh bronze growth, the gum trees looked regal. And wattles dotted the slope with bright yellow. Clayton bent down and ran his hands through the field. His fingers brushed the seed heads and grain sprinkled to the ground—plump and full.

Waringa stood. As he did so, the field of wheat withered and retreated into the earth. "It is there. Waiting."

"Bring it back," said Clayton. "If you can make Paddle Creek flourish, why am I bothering?"

"It is just an illusion. A shimmer in the heat haze. A promise of the hope to come."

"Promises?" Clayton scoffed. "Your word means nothing. You said the weapon would work –"

"I said it might," clarified Waringa.

"You said the serpent would give me answers, and it just vanished, shrivelled up. It upset Mum."

"It did give you answers. You just need to find the right spell. And it wouldn't have caused grief if you hadn't attacked it."

Ignoring Waringa's convenient explanation, Clayton looked out to the hills. "It's too far. I can't free the rain spirits or face the Red King. I'm not cut-out for this."

"You are the only one who can do this. Do you think your mother is capable?"

Clayton sighed and turned towards his house.

"Where are you going?" asked Waringa. "Don't give up."

"I'm not," said Clayton. "But if I'm going to the hills, I'll need food and water." He wandered towards the house and froze.

Outside sat the local copper's four-wheel drive.

Clayton scurried out of the open and hunkered behind the bulldozer. "I knew I was in trouble."

Waringa stood behind him, gazing towards the hills. "We shouldn't dawdle. Your parents may have already decided on Rusty's fate."

Clayton tugged at Waringa's paw. "Get down. They might come out here and see you."

"Would they believe it, if they did see me?"

He had to admit that Waringa had a point. "Look, they're going."

The local copper came out of the house, heading towards his car, talking to Walter. The dry wind carried their voices away from him, but Walter pointed across the paddock and the policeman leaned into his vehicle and picked up the UHF.

Clayton wished he could hear what they were saying. He wished he knew how much trouble he was in, but Dad's face didn't give anything away.

The copper rested his hand on Walter's shoulder and bowed his head. They exchanged more words before he got in his car and drove off. Walter climbed into the ute and tore off in the opposite direction.

Clayton wondered if his mum was home. "Hopefully the coast is clear," said Clayton, turning to Waringa. "Come on."

Clayton snuck across the garden and crept up to the front door.

The rope had been tossed to one side. There was nothing serpentine about it anymore. Clayton's subconscious regurgitated the image of rope hanging from the rafter. The memory caught in his throat, and pounded on his chest. "I don't want to remember again," he said, struggling for breath. "Get it out of my head, Waringa." Tears rolled down Clayton's cheeks before he even realised he was crying. "Waringa?" He turned when the fox didn't answer. "Waringa?" But the fox had gone.

Clayton curled up on the front step, hugging his knees to his chest. "I can't do it." He wasn't the warrior his dad was. Dad wouldn't be scared of dust and flames towering towards him. Dad wouldn't be sitting here crying. Crying was weak, so he always said. The porch came into focus as he wiped the tears from his eyes. On the far side of the deck, the sunlight shimmered on the surface of the water in Rusty's bowl. Clayton dabbed his wet cheeks with the bottom of his t-shirt and got to his feet.

Taking a deep breath, he slowly opened the door. No noise filtered from inside. Treading lightly, he made his way along the hallway and stopped when he reached the kitchen.

His mum was asleep in the chair. Her head rested on the kitchen table with one hand draped on the mobile phone. Tangled hair fell over her face.

He wanted to wake her, tell her everything would be okay, tell her Dad would be okay. He pulled back a strand of hair from her face, and she snored softly.

"There is no time for day-dreaming," a voice whispered from behind him.

Startled, Clayton spun around.

Waringa padded around the room, his footsteps making no noise. The fox was so tall now that he needed to duck under the doorway.

"You came here for supplies, so get them and let's go."

Clayton held a finger up to his lips and mouthed "Shhh."

He tiptoed to the fridge and, placing his fingers on the rubber seal, pried the door ajar. Despite his smooth movement, the bottles in the fridge rattled as he opened the door and the old refrigerator ozone smell wafted into the room.

Mum took a deep shuddering breath.

Clayton froze, not daring to breathe.

A strand of hair fell back over her face as her normal breathing resumed.

Waringa pointed to the fridge.

"Right," whispered Clayton. There was little in here except for a few cans of soft drink and Dad's beer. Clayton grabbed two cans of lemonade and closed the fridge gently. From the adjacent cupboard, he plucked a packet of choc-chip biscuits from the shelf.

"Okay, let's go," said Waringa.

"In a minute." Clayton snuck into the living room. His bag was on the couch. Someone had emptied the contents out. School books and his diary lay scattered on the coffee table. He snatched the bag and filled it with the drinks and biscuits.

"Okay, can we go now?" pleaded Waringa. "Before your mum wakes up and stops you."

"In a second." Clayton pushed the couch towards the cabinet. He hopped up and reached for the keys on top.

"What are you doing? The key should still be in the quad where you left it," said Waringa. "You don't need Walter's key for the quad bike."

"I know." Clayton unlocked the cabinet and reached inside.

"No," said Waringa. "You don't need that. That's going too far." He padded to Clayton's side.

Clayton looked up into his amber eyes. "We can't just free the rain spirits. We need to defeat the Red King once and for all." He grabbed the barrel of the rifle and pulled it out slowly.

"Do you even know how to use it?"

Clayton reached into the ammunition box in the bottom of the cabinet. "I've seen Davo and Dad use it."

"If you take that, I won't come with you."

"Fine. Go. Nothing you've suggested has worked anyway," said Clayton, pocketing the ammunition. "I don't care what you tell me anymore. I'm going to defeat him at any cost."

CHAPTER 12

By the time Clayton returned to the quad, the sun had begun to seep into the earth. As it kissed the horizon, the soil's cracked parched lips bled ochre blood across the plains. Land and saltbush and fence posts glimmered gold and orange.

He threw his school bag into the trailer and carefully placed the rifle beside it. He hadn't seen or heard any sign of Waringa since he'd left the house, and the silence had deepened. No cockatoos or corellas squawked like they normally did during this time of day; no sheep bleated in the paddocks; no small birds chatted and twittered among the saltbush. It was silent. Everyone had left him. In his heart, he knew Waringa wasn't coming back this time. Not that Waringa had been any help anyway, nor the spear or the serpent Clayton had spent his time chasing. At least this time, he had a real weapon. The kind of weapon Dad would use.

The key still sat in the ignition. Clayton was surprised and relieved when the quad started on the first go, grumbling as if it were trying to cough up a fur ball. The engine noise comforted Clayton, as did the rattling of the trailer as he drove across the paddock towards Davo's property and the hills beyond.

Up ahead, jagged shapes glistened like tin foil on Davo's homestead. Clayton had no idea what the shapes were, but bathed in the fading sunlight it looked like an amber halo surrounded the bluestone building.

As he approached, he realised the gate had been closed again. With the latch broken, a strand of baling twine tied the gate to the post. Had Dad been back here looking for him?

Clayton scanned up ahead but there was no sign of his dad's ute. He jumped from the quad, undid the baling twine and threw the pink string in the trailer.

Clayton drove slowly up the track, keeping an eye out for any sign of his dad. As he came up alongside the house, the quad stuttered and ground to a halt. He tried turning the key again, but it wouldn't tick over. It sounded like the guts had been kicked out of it. He tried again. The grunting didn't sound like it did before, it sounded more like the battery had died or it was out of . . . fuel. Of course! He'd driven kilometres since he'd last filled up. Climbing off, he lifted the bonnet. Sure enough, the tank was bone dry.

Clayton turned to Davo's house. It was possible there was still fuel in the garage, but panic rippled through him at the thought of entering the house again.

In the fading light, the hills were layers of purple and grey. Davo's property was as vast as theirs was, and the hills were some distance beyond that.

Davo had got them stuck in the middle of his property once, and it'd taken them half the day to walk back to his place and return with fuel.

"You ever feel like you're running on empty?" Davo had asked as they walked back to the house.

"I don't understand. What do you mean?"

"Like the magic has drained from your tank."

Clayton shrugged. He hadn't understood at the time. As he walked up the stairs to Davo's front porch, he still wasn't entirely sure that he did.

Why, Davo? Why did you leave us?

Dozens of rocks were dotted across the front porch. They weren't here before. He looked around and realised that the jagged shapes he'd seen glinting in the light were from the windows. Every pane of glass had been smashed. Cracks ran through one window, on another only a few shards clung to the windowpane.

Had Dad done this? Clayton peered through one of the windows. It was getting darker by the minute, but there didn't appear to be any sign of movement. Taking a breath, he walked inside and towards the garage door.

As he reached the steps leading down to the garage, dread pounded in his bones and muscles, making it difficult to stand. Why didn't his parents tell him how Davo died? Why did the image of him hanging there surface from his memory?

Clayton clasped his head in his hands, trying to suppress the memory, but as he stood on the top step to the garage, he couldn't get the image out of his head. He couldn't save Davo. But he could still make it rain for his dad.

He balled his fists, fingernails digging into his palms like razors so he could concentrate on the pain instead of his fear. Taking a deep breath, he shook out his hands and walked down the steps.

The last rays from the setting sun filtered in through the window, highlighting the cardboard boxes, tools and broken furniture littering the garage floor, along with a couple of unlabelled jerry cans. Davo had never been the most organised person in the world.

Clayton kept his eyes plastered to the garage floor and its contents. Although he knew the rope was no longer there, a tiny part of him wanted to look to see if it jogged his memory.

"No, I don't. Focus on the ground," he insisted to himself.

A red jerry can and a black one sat against the far wall. Last time Davo filled up the quad it was from a metal jerry can. Clayton lifted them both. The red was half empty and the black too heavy for him to lift.

"What's the bet the black one is the one I need?" Clayton said to himself. He unscrewed the cap of the black jerry can and sniffed the strong scent of diesel. In the other, the smell was sweeter, but it looked too viscous to be petrol. Maybe it was two-stroke. He didn't know whether it would work but he was out of options: the light was fading and the walls of the garage loomed inwards, creeping in on him. He needed to get out of here.

He grabbed the red jerry can and walked backwards, dragging it across the garage floor with two hands. His calves bumped into something solid. He dropped the can and turned. A chair sat in the middle of the room under the rafters. Why hadn't he noticed it before? And why was there a chair in the garage?

The memory flooded back to him like a tidal wave, knocking him in the guts. No one had answered the door. He'd got the key. He'd wandered inside. He'd seen the note on the kitchen table. He hadn't understood. Rusty had been barking and pawing at the garage door. A crash of wood breaking resonated from behind the door. Scared, he'd walked to the garage. Why didn't he sprint?

Davo's eyes were wide; his legs kicked spasmodically; his face turned a ghastly shade of blue. Clayton had tried to lift Davo up but couldn't reach his legs. The chair underneath Davo had broken, the spindly wooden leg snapped off. Clayton raced to the kitchen and grabbed another. By the time he returned there was no kicking and twitching. He'd stood on the chair. He'd tried to reach the rope. He'd tried to lift him up. He'd tried and failed. He'd been too weak.

"It was my fault." He came back to the present at the sound of his own voice and found himself sitting on the floor, sobbing and hugging his knees.

He looked up. The rope wasn't there, but there was a line on the rafters where the varnish had rubbed off. Clayton heaved. The taste of bile filled his mouth.

He pushed to his feet, lugged the jerry can across the floor and out the house.

This happened last time. He'd fled. Davo's blue lips and limp body was hanging there and he'd fled seeking the fresh air outside on the porch. Dazed and in shock, he stumbled into a web at the top of the porch stairs, freaked out as sticky strands suffocated him, and tripped down the stairs. Clayton remembered walking in a blur with a sore head and arriving back home late where his mum had sat him down and told him the news.

"I can't be here. It was all my fault. I can't be here." The same dizziness and shock consumed him now.

He ran to the quad, tipped every drop of fuel out, but it barely filled a quarter of the tank. He uncoupled the trailer to reduce the drag and took his backpack and the rifle out. Dad had taken the arm sling off the rifle long ago, complaining it got in the way. Real men carried their rifles in their hands not on their shoulders like a handbag, Dad always said. But the swivels were still there. Clayton grabbed the baling twine from the trailer and tied it through the two swivels, making a pseudo-strap. It wasn't the most fashionable look, but he slung the rifle over his shoulder along with his backpack and crossed his fingers as he turned over the ignition. The quad bike started reluctantly, but at least it was going and he was grateful he didn't have to prime the fuel lines.

Clayton flicked the headlights on to guide his way in the growing darkness and he tore along Davo's paddock, hoping to make up time, but more than anything he just wanted to escape the old homestead and its memories.

He veered onto a track, whizzing past the saltbush feedlot. Soon he was driving across open country dotted sporadically with brittle bluebush. Twigs crunched under the tyres, and after a while the bushes started closing in on each side like arms grasping to slow his progress. They scratched the side of the quad and prickled his legs as the shrubbery encroached upon the track.

Clayton veered and swerved to avoid bushes halting his path and soon there was no trace of the track at all. Even with the quad's headlights shining ahead, it was difficult to make out the terrain. He considered stopping for a break on more than one occasion, but out alone in the dark with no one around for kilometres he felt exposed: inside and out.

As he continued driving, he looked up towards the hills. They appeared closer. Surely, he must be near the back of his brother's property by now. From there he could jump the fence onto the conservation reserve at the base of the hills.

Despite his conviction that he was getting closer, there was an uneasy feeling growing in his stomach. Light-headed, he rubbed his eyes. The shrubs in the headlights blurred and danced across the paddock.

The ground became stonier, and the quad bumped over the rocky terrain. Shallow rivulets appeared in the soil crust in front of him. They turned into a pattern like veins spanning as far as the headlights could shine. He hadn't been up this far on Davo's property for a long time. It didn't look familiar. He looked for the hills, but all he saw in the beam of the headlights were flat plains. Had he turned the quad around somehow? How did he get lost on his brother's land?

The engine grumbled and spluttered. He levered the quad into neutral and revved the accelerator.

"Don't stall. Don't stall," he pleaded, as fear rose in his stomach. "Please, don't leave me stuck here."

Revving the accelerator again, the engine ceased stuttering, and he drove off. Too scared it would never start again, he sped up and clutched the handlebars tight.

Four beams of light reflected off the stones and soil crust. Four beams? Dizziness overcame him. Two channels ran parallel in front of him instead of the vein-like pattern before. Was he seeing double? Clayton strained his eyes to focus. The quad jolted. The front left wheel fell, stopping the vehicle in its tracks, and the force flung him sideways. Before he knew it, he was tumbling down a slope. The landing knocked the breath out of him, and his knees and palms hit stones, sending pins and needles down his limbs. He rubbed his hands. They were grazed and he touched sticky blood. Next to him, the edge of an embankment towered; a few feet above him, the quad's headlights gazed obliquely across the paddock and night sky.

The headlights dimmed, casting shadows around him.

In the distance, a pair of white eyes shone in the headlights.

"Waringa?" He instantly regretted calling out. Was that really him? Those eyes weren't amber like Waringa's. More pairs of eyes appeared. Dozens of white eyes crept across the plain towards him. Clayton strived for breath. He stood and backed towards the side of the bank. Patting the embankment with his sore hands, he discovered the slope was almost vertical. He jimmied his foot into a nook in the side of the sheer face and reached to the edge of the bank. Soil crumbled under his fingers and he slid back down.

"Waringa?" Please let it be him. He thought of shining the torch on the newcomers before realising he'd left it in the trailer.

There were dozens of eyes now; the nearest creature was a few metres from the quad bike above him.

Clouds streamed across the sky, concealing the light of the stars.

A whooping noise echoed above him, and lights panned the ground a few kilometres to his right. A tiny part of him hoped it was his dad in a helicopter. Dad would find him and make everything okay again, but the lights continued off into the distance and the darkness deepened once more.

The quad's headlights blinked out, and the white eyes disappeared into the night. Clayton reached for his rifle only to find it gone, along with his backpack. They must have fallen off his shoulder when he fell. He patted the ground, finding only soil and stones. He shivered despite the balmy night air. Picking up a rock, he crouched with his back against the embankment and waited.

CHAPTER 13

He stayed awake for hours looking for the white-eyed creatures, but there was no sign of them. Exhaustion must've eventually taken hold for he was suddenly fishing with Davo and Dad. Davo showed Clayton how to skim rocks across the river; while Rusty, still an awkward and excited puppy, chased moths fluttering on the banks. As real as it felt, Clayton knew it was a dream. Not only was Davo here, but Dad was smiling.

"You gotta get down low, Clay, buddy," said Davo.

Clayton hurled a rock. It plonked in the middle of the stream.

"Ha!" Dad chuckled.

Davo removed his Akubra and hung it on a tree branch overhanging the river. "Reckon you can do better, Dad?" Davo goaded.

Dad stuck his fishing rod in the soft bank and took his time plucking the flattest and smoothest stone he could find from the riverside.

"Watch an expert, Clay." Dad slung the stone and it crashed into the water like a brick.

"Good job," mocked Davo, standing with his arms crossed over his chest. "Face it, Dad, you're a farmer. You work your magic on the land, not on water."

Rusty barked in acknowledgment.

"Clay, on the other hand, is a master of water. He's caught twice as many fish as you, Dad."

"Here." Davo handed Clayton a shiny flat stone. "This one will work its magic."

"Magic?"

"Command it to skim the surface, like a spell. Words have power."

Clayton whispered to the stone, but he couldn't hear his own voice. It was like he was watching the scene from afar. He saw himself fling the stone. It ricocheted twice across the surface before sinking into the water. Then he was the stone. Sinking. Water surrounded him, lapping and swirling, and he was drowning. Fish darted past him like torpedos, their white eyes glaring at him through the murky darkness of the river. White eyes? He knew that meant something, but fishing with Davo and Dad relaxed him. He didn't want to remember. The fish started flicking their tails rhythmically, thumping them against the water with a sound like footsteps. Footsteps?

Clayton snapped out of his dream. The sky was already a predawn grey, and he found himself lying on the ground, staring into the snotty nose of a Merino sheep. Ignoring Clayton's presence, it ambled along and nuzzled a rock covered with algae.

Algae? Nearby, it sounded like waves were washing upon a shore. Confused and disorientated, Clayton sat up and rubbed his ribs where stones had been digging into his side. He was in a rocky creek bed. The dry, exposed bed was dotted with sheep. More Merinos stood on the top of the bank, nibbling whatever tufts of grass survived.

They must've wandered onto Davo's land with the gate open. He should've been worried that his dad would go troppo; but as he looked along the streambed, he realised where he was. He'd passed the rocky floodplains and fallen down the bank of Paddle Creek. He wasn't too far from the source of the creek. And therefore the hills.

The sun already stung, and a breeze funnelled in Clayton's direction. Would the heat and wind bring the Red King out? The thought prompted him to get moving. He stood shakily and looked around for the quad bike.

Directly above him, the quad was tilted on its side, the bonnet dangled precariously over the edge of the bank. He looked at his grazed knees and palms, astonished nothing seemed broken. He was even more thankful the quad bike hadn't toppled over the edge and landed on top of him.

A dozen sheep cluttered around the quad, perhaps hopeful he'd brought hay. The edge of the bank was in reach, but the slope was too steep to climb up where he'd landed. Clayton walked along the creek to a shallower section of the river. As he scrambled up the side of the bank, the sheep bleated persistently.

"I haven't got any food," he said as he walked up to the quad. They didn't accept his explanation and crowded around him.

Grabbing the side rim of the quad bike, he tried to pull it upright, but the metal dug into his fingers and the vehicle refused to budge. The thing must've weighed half a tonne. Dad or Davo might've been able to pull it upright.

In the dawn light, tiers of purple and grey hills towered nearby. He was closer than he thought. Surely, it was possible to walk the rest of the way.

Down in the channel, something clanked under the hooves of one of the sheep. Clayton noticed the can of soft drink lying on its side along with his backpack splayed on a rock.

"Great." He clambered back down into the creek bed and scavenged among the rocks for his belongings. His packet of biscuits had split open and scattered, the choc chips indistinguishable from the dirt. He picked one up and tried to brush the dirt off, but it only served to smear the dirt into the food more. One can of drink lay punctured by a jagged rock. The other drink was nowhere to be seen. Nor could he see the rifle. The thought of being defenceless made his guts ache. Or was that just hunger? He tipped the can up and savoured the last few drops of fluid that remained. The tiny amount of soft drink made his stomach ache with thirst and hunger more than it had before. There hardly seemed any point taking his backpack now.

He continued along the channel. If he followed the creek bed, it should take him directly to its source. A few sheep followed, but soon must've realised they weren't going to get any food, as they quickly resumed foraging along the bank.

Around the first meander, the creek banks turned to ironstone, and tucked away in the rocks a tiny pool of water persisted, no bigger or deeper than a kids' wading pool. The stagnant water stank like wet clothes that had been left in the washing machine too long; and in the wind, the water lapped gently over the rocky creek bed, wafting the stench towards him.

It was quiet except for the faint murmur of the water as it lapped against the shore in the morning breeze. On the edge of the water lay the rifle. The makeshift strap had snapped, and the baling twine blew in the breeze. He picked it up, retied the strings and slung it over his shoulder.

How had it flown so far when he fell? Had the Red King sent enemies to hide it from him? Maybe the eyes last night weren't just sheep.

The thought stayed with him as the morning progressed. As the day warmed up, the thought of the Red King striking while he was alone dwelled heavy on his conscious. The sun crept through the cleft of the hills, illuminating the creek bed. Golden river pebbles glistened as if Midas had touched every stone.

"Magic," he muttered to himself. The scenery filled him with a glimpse of hope. Words. All he needed were words. That's what Davo had said in his dream, that magic was just words. A spell to defeat the Red King. With renewed optimism, Clayton walked faster.

The creek gradually deepened and became rockier and more difficult to navigate. He climbed the bank again and stared towards the hills. They didn't look any closer. The second row of hills dwarfed the first and the third dwarfed the entire landscape. And the sun was already high in the sky.

As he continued walking, flies droned and clambered onto his arms and legs. Across the paddock, cockatoos squawked and stripped bark off a withered eucalypt on the side of the bank. Noise intensified and dizziness filled his head. Parched, his throat burned, and his tongue kept sticking to the roof of his mouth.

He sat on the side of the rocky bank and rested his head in his hands. Above him, the blinding yellow orb hung restlessly, moving faster than it should. Salt-encrusted soil along the edges of the bank glinted like quartz under its gaze. Clayton squinted, wishing he'd brought his sunnies.

The breeze escalated, kicking dust into the air and creating a haze in the distance. An intangible gloom lingered in the sky despite the sun's glare. Did the Red King know Clayton was coming?

Amid the dust haze, he saw a line. He strained his eyes. It was Davo's boundary fence. Beyond that, the hills were dotted with grey saltbush and bands of spinifex grass.

A whooping shattered the air. Roaring above, a helicopter hovered slowly along the creek's flanks.

"No, not now. I'm so close."

Clayton ran. His knees and ankles jarred against the compacted earth and his head spun, but he needed to find shelter before they found him. A mob of kangaroos bounded alongside him, fleeing the helicopter.

Amazed that they hadn't spotted him, Clayton reached the fence. Perfectly intact, the tall Ringlock fence was topped with two strands of barbwire. There was no way he could get over or through it. Even Dad, as tall as he was, would've struggled to straddle it. Clayton searched for a gate but saw little through the haze.

Alongside him, there was a deep twang and vibration of wire. The kangaroos? They always found a way underneath. A few metres to his right, a large buck squeezed beneath the fence. Catching its fur along the bottom barb, the kangaroo strummed the bottom wire and the fence jolted between the star droppers.

If a roo could squeeze underneath, so could he. He darted to the ditch under the fence and crouched down. The chopping noise receded in volume. Gazing up, he realised the helicopter had veered towards the eastern edge of the paddock. Why hadn't they spotted him? A thought curdled in his brain. He realised the dust had thickened and obscured him from the helicopter's view.

As the bellowing roar of the rotor blades dissipated, he heard it.

Laughter.

Even though the helicopter was gone, the roos were still fleeing, bounding up the hillside. It wasn't the helicopter they were escaping from.

CHAPTER 14

The Red King drifted across the paddock.

Clayton ducked under the fence, prying his body into the ditch the kangaroos had created. The barbwire caught a strand of his hair and pulled it from its roots. He flattened down on his stomach. As he tried to drag himself along the dirt, the barbwire jagged on the rifle.

How stupid. Why hadn't he taken it off first? The sun blazed on the back of his calves, or was that the Red King's heat? Sand grains stung his legs. He tried to wriggle underneath, but the more he squirmed the more the rifle caught on the wire.

"Why do you persist?" the Red King cackled.

Stuck on his stomach, Clayton tried to look over his shoulder at the demon, but all he saw was haze. He choked on the dust as it stung his eyes. He buried his head in his arms.

Wind blew against Clayton's ankles like a blowtorch. The heat was agonising and every time he lifted his head, he felt like he was swallowing a paddock full of topsoil. He knew he couldn't stay here.

He felt for the rifle, grabbed the barrel hanging over his shoulder and tugged desperately. The gun finally dislodged, making the barbwire reverberate and dragging it across his legs, leaving a graze. Still disorientated and blinded by dust, he struggled under the fence and sprang to his feet.

He squinted, using his hand to shield his eyes from the sun and blowing sand. Beyond the fence a willy-willy scoured the banks. The Red King's face was just visible in the accumulating dust.

Could he try a spell? If a spell would free the rain spirits it might defeat the Red King. But what words? He couldn't just ask him to go away and come again another day.

"*Abracadabra*," Clayton whispered, knowing in his heart it wouldn't be that easy.

The Red King bellowed with a derisive laugh. It whipped up small pebbles from the creek bed and flung them in Clayton's direction.

"*Disappearus! Go-us away-us.*" His cheeks flushed the colour of the surrounding dust.

A rock collided with his shin, breaking the skin. Clayton cried out. Another stone flew past, missing his cheek by inches, and collided with the rocks behind him. The sound of stone hitting stone rang out like a gun shot. The rifle! He removed the sling from his shoulder and fumbled in his pocket for the ammunition.

"Really?" The Red King's mocking voice cut through the noise of the wind. "Haven't you learned yet?" Its face was clearly visible, but the dust continued swirling around the demon's body. "Even if you defeat me, nothing will change."

"Yes it will. I'll free the rain spirits and it'll rain and everything will be okay again." Clayton pointed the rifle at the Red King. "Dad keeps saying so."

"Does your father tell you how to undo the safety catch?"

Clayton looked down. As he did so, a gust of wind swept up his legs and pounded him in the chest, knocking him off his feet and flat on his back. He clasped his chest, winded and out of breath.

The Red King hurled stones against the ground, sparks ignited, and a spinifex tussock burst into flames.

Grasping the rifle tight, Clayton darted up the hill, dodging stones, sticks, and other debris as they ricocheted against the rocky hill face. Hot dust stung his nostrils, but he didn't dare look back.

He scrambled along the rocky edge of the dry creek bed

winding its way through a cleft in the hills. Along the bank, skeletal trees with white bark creaked in the Red King's gusty breath. Clayton thought that at any moment the Red King would blow so hard the trees would drop their limbs on him.

With hands grazed, Clayton painfully grabbed onto the tree branches and pulled himself up the hill.

The force of the Red King's breath subsided. Exhausted, Clayton paused to look back down the hill. A willy-willy swirled, skirting around the base of the hills.

Clayton sat on a rocky outcrop and tried to concentrate. Waringa had said the rain spirits were in the hills, but where?

The wind eased and the heat began to overcome him. The back of his legs and neck were drenched with sweat. With the stillness of the air and the sun pounding on the rocks, the extent of his exhaustion began to set in. His body ached; his head spun; and his throat felt as if it were on fire.

Alongside him, veins of quartzite broke up a slab of rust coloured ironstone. In the dry soil between the rocks, spinifex grass dotted the slopes like pincushions; and ghostly gum trees had shed all leaves. Even they were feeling the heat.

There was no sign of the Red King on the plains below. But like the flames in the hay bales, maybe he was here in disguise.

Though the metal of the rifle burned Clayton's hand, he held on, waiting for the Red King to show himself. But there was no wind, only oppressive heat. Moistening his lips with his tongue, he tasted blood and realised his lips were cracked and blistered. He looked for the nearest tree and huddled in the narrow line of shade emerging from its trunk. The unsympathetic shadow slinked silently across the rock escarpment and shrank as if the tree sucked it up into its bark.

Clayton looked up. The sun hadn't moved. There was no reason for the shadows to move so quickly. Unless the Red King's heat was scaring even the shadows away.

In the distance, a faint cackling laugh cut through the silence.

He wasted no time in continuing further along the riverbed up into the hills. The banks on either side became steeper, towering over his head like skyscrapers.

He stopped looking around and focused on the ground, partly to make sure he found a secure footing and partly to distract himself from the seemingly never-ending creek bed. The ground underfoot gradually changed from small jagged rocks to boulders that he had to jump between. Sunbaking skinks scurried for shelter as he passed.

Soon shade fell upon him. He looked up. The creek rose vertical like a short cliff. He recalled seeing a mini waterfall in the hills when he and Davo had come exploring three years ago.

There was at least a metre of shade at the base of the waterfall. Clayton took off his rifle and pressed his back against the cliff. The rocks were cool against his exposed skin. Exhausted, he slumped onto a smooth boulder and stretched out his legs. He must be close to the start of the creek now; he was sure this waterfall had been near the headwaters the last time.

Seeking relief for his burned skin, he pressed the back of his arms against the rocks. Shutting his eyes, he tried to picture the time when he and Davo paddled in the coolness of the waterhole. There had been a tyre swing dangling from an overhanging lush gum tree and water deep enough to do bombs in the middle and splash each other. And a shallow cave you could crawl into if you were game enough to duck your head under the waterfall. With the water level low, the cave must be further up the cliff now. Clayton opened his eyes to glance up at the cave, and to where the tyre swing used to be. The gum tree held but a few leaves, bronzing mistletoe, and a frayed rope. The sight of the rope reminded him of Davo hanging from the rafters. He shut his eyes again and tried to block it out.

His ankles suddenly burned; even through his shoes the heat seared his feet. He opened his eyes. The shadow had continued to shrink unnaturally quickly. The rocks below heated up, baking him like a trout in a bamboo steamer.

"Where are you?" he called out. "I know you're here."

The Red King's chuckle echoed on the distant breeze. "There is nowhere for you to run. Nowhere to hide."

Clayton swung the rifle over his shoulder. Roaring echoed further down the creek. A brown mass came into focus. Hot dust swirled like a cyclone, scouring the sides of the creek bank, dislodging pebbles and dirt and hurling them into the air. Sticks, the size of Clayton's arms, tore from trees and were sucked into the storm.

Clayton stared up at the dry waterfall. There were small holes to cram his feet into. He took a deep breath, jimmied his foot in a small recess and reached his arm up. His fingers found a crumbly ledge of rock.

"I've got to be mad," he muttered as a sprinkling of rubble rained down to the creek bed.

The shade began to retreat up the face of the waterfall. He continued climbing, but soon the rocks were like embers to the touch. He tried to climb faster to beat the retreating shade, but the thought of the boulders below convinced him to take his time. The cave he remembered must be only a few feet above.

The thunderous howling of the Red King drowned out all other noise. The demon must be close, but Clayton was too scared to look behind him or down.

A stick collided with the rock face just above his head, sending dirt, rocks and splinters of wood tumbling down. Clayton pressed his body close to the rocks and ducked his head to avoid the falling debris.

He found another foothold and propelled himself onto a narrow ledge in front of the cave. Too exhausted to sit, he huddled as close to the cave entrance as possible and dared to look down.

The thundering ceased and the Red King stopped attacking. Its face jutted out from the dust a few metres below Clayton.

"You won't go in there." There was desperation in the Red King's voice, as if it were pleading.

Was this it? Was this the start of the watercourse – the place where the rain spirits were hiding?

Cobwebs and fibrous roots spanned the entrance like they had at Davo's house. Inside was so dark, the gloom so deep.

"You are no warrior."

Clayton propped himself onto his hands and knees. On the ledge, a bone dug into his palm. Possibly the skeleton of a rock wallaby that'd lost its footing. He hoped. He hated to think of the alternatives.

"I can sense your fear. Your father might say Hoppers are tough, but you . . . " it chuckled, "you are weak."

Clayton used the skeleton to wipe away the cobwebs and shuffled into the cool shadows of the cave.

"You can't free the rain spirits. You don't have it in you." The Red King's voice drifted off as Clayton crawled further into the darkness.

He could see less than a metre in front of his face. Claustrophobia set in and his chest tightened. Up ahead, the roof became lower. As kids, they'd never been brave enough to explore the cave fully. Even Davo had chickened out. It could be a dead end, and he would end up stuck here until the Red King gave up. *If* the Red King ever gave up.

Clayton lowered his body and nudged his way forward. The further he went, the darker it became. He felt forward with his hands. A jagged rock like a stalactite dangled from the ceiling, leaving a small gap. Clayton slunk onto his belly and dragged his body along. He reached his hands into the darkness beyond and attempted to pull himself further. His body didn't move.

Panic set in. His heart rate quickened; beads of sweat formed on his temples, and air danced around his mouth, refusing to enter his lungs.

"Help." The word caught in his throat as he tried to scream. *Dad, help me.* What was he thinking? Dad was nowhere nearby. He'd never find him in here. Clayton would end up stuck until he starved to death. He started to gasp, convinced someone had sucked the air from the cave. He wriggled forward in desperation.

"Dad!" he cried through gasping sobs. "Waringa! Please, I need you." He lay there for what seemed like forever until crying gave him a headache and gasping made his lungs hurt.

"Come on. Calm down, Clayton," he said aloud. "Think logically."

He took a deep breath and tried to shuffle backwards to where the roof was higher. Scraping of metal against rock screeched above him. The rifle! He shuffled back more, and the rifle dislodged from the rock. He'd forgotten *again* that it was on his shoulders.

You idiot, he told himself. He took the rifle off and looked to the cave entrance. Why hadn't he shot the Red King when he had a chance?

Why did he come in here? He could go out again, into the open air where the breeze would cool his sweaty skin. It would be so much easier to retreat away from this cramped stuffy darkness.

"I have to go on." Saying it aloud gave him a smidgeon of confidence.

He pushed the rifle ahead of him through the small gap and lay as low as possible, still uncertain whether he'd fit through. He dragged his body through the darkness. The cave ceiling scraped his back. He paused, tempted to retreat. He lifted his hands and tapped the ceiling. It felt like it became higher just ahead. He sucked in his stomach and wiggled forward. His hand touched damp ground. The darkness eased. He could see at least a few feet in front of him now. Soon the roof was high enough to kneel again. The damp rocks cooled his legs. Clayton crawled further into an open section of the cave. It was smaller than his bedroom and barely high enough for him to stand but compared to the confined space earlier it was blissfully spacious and smelled earthy and sweet.

Clayton stood and tapped his feet on the rocky floor. Water splashed underfoot. It was brighter than it had been before and as he looked around, he realised why. A beam of sunlight filtered from a small crack in the roof, casting light on a man hunched in the far corner of the cave.

He bent down, picked up the rifle and pointed it in the man's direction. "Who are you?"

The figure didn't respond.

Clayton crept closer. The slit of light shone upon a wooden bodice and face, which was covered in carvings etched into the wood.

"It's just a sculpture."

The sculpture sat on a rock with its feet digging into the ground. Clayton prodded it with the end of his rifle. The man's eyes were hollowed out, his mouth nothing but a cavern of wood. Moss dotted his arms and legs, and tree roots dangled through the crack in the cave's ceiling like a curtain of hair.

Clayton looked back at the narrow gap he'd crawled through to get here. The thought of going back made his skin crawl. "Now what?" he said to himself.

Creaking, like tree branches grating against each other, resonated behind him.

The wooden man turned his head towards Clayton with jerky movements.

"Must you leave so soon?"

Clayton staggered and struck the back of his skull on the ceiling. He clasped his head as pain shot to his temples and white light filled his vision. "Huh?" he said, refocusing on the wooden man.

"What purpose have you here?" The hollow eyes glowed sky blue.

Clayton rubbed his head. "I've come to kill the Red King so it can rain again on Dad's farm."

"Kill?" asked the wooden figure. "You cannot kill him. The Red King will always exist, as will I."

"I have to kill him. Waringa promised. He promised rain. He promised everything would be okay. Dad needs rain."

Above him, something rumbled and dirt rained down from the gap in the cave.

The wooden man didn't seem to care. "Waringa told you what you needed to hear. He made you do what you needed to do. Now all you have to do is say what needs to be said. Magic can still send water from the hills."

The rumbling grew louder.

"What is that?" asked Clayton, gazing upwards.

"He's angry. So angry. So much pent-up rage and suppressed emotion."

The ceiling began to crumble. Pebbles tinkled against the wooden man's head.

"Go out there and use your magic. You must face him head-on and release me," said the man.

"I can't. It's hot and I'm so tired."

"There is only you. So many others have tried, but they are not warriors."

"Neither am I. I'm weak," muttered Clayton.

The tree roots dangling above extended further towards the man. The roots wrapped tight around the wooden man's legs and travelled up his body. "You're running out of time," he said.

"What magic do I need?"

The man didn't respond. More tree roots grew downwards, binding his wrists and gagging his mouth with fibrous strands.

Clayton looked up at the gap in the ceiling and yelled. "I know it's you up there. Let him go!" He yanked at the tree roots. "Stop it!"

The roots refused to budge. They dug into the man's wooden skin so tightly it was hard to tell if they were tree roots or part of his body; like veins, the roots traversed the length of his limbs.

More descended from the ceiling. The crack in the roof widened. Rocks and dirt tumbled down, and more sunlight poured into the cave, heating the ground. The moisture on the rocks at his feet evaporated. The humidity became suffocating. And the roots travelled further up the man's body, wrapping around his neck.

"No. Stop!" Clayton cried. He tugged desperately at the tree roots.

Roots sprawled along the ground and prodded Clayton's foot. He backed away hastily, tripping over a rock.

Fibrous roots spread over his rifle. Clayton crawled along the cave floor, avoiding the roots dangling from the ceiling and dodged the tentacle-like taproot worming over the ground. He grabbed a sharp rock and sliced the root away from the gun. Fine roots tickled his fingers, but he kept on slicing and hacking away at the timber.

Freeing his weapon, he turned back to the man. More rubble and dirt tumbled into the cave, and although light filtered inside, claustrophobia came over him. He looked at the narrow entrance. Roots began to clog the tiny space, closing the gap.

Rifle in hand, he scrambled up the torso of the wooden man, towards the crack of light, praying he'd fit through.

Clayton pulled rocks and scraped dirt away from the tree root, trying to make room to squeeze through. As he did so, dust trickled into the cave like a stream. It stung his eyes and clogged his hair.

Throwing the rifle up through the hole, he grasped a tree root and pulled himself out of the cave up onto a wide plateau with a scattering of trees and clumps of spinifex. He lugged himself to the shade of a tree and collapsed.

CHAPTER 15

When he came to, there was no shade. No clouds roamed across the sky, and the sun pounded down with intense loathing. But there was also no demon.

Clayton looked around. From here, a network of shallow rills – all bone dry – fed into the waterfall. They spanned across the plateau like veins. It reminded Clayton of Mars with its ochre rock, and where there weren't rocks there was the odd brittle plant.

Arched away from the prevailing winds as if doubled over in pain, gum trees grew through the rock. Short and rotund, they looked more like self-pruned bonsais.

Clayton wandered to the far side of the plateau. A swag of flies followed, clinging to his sweat. There was nothing here except more dirt and a sheer hundred-metre drop to jagged rocks below.

Riding high on the thermals, a wedge-tailed eagle circled the peaks. For a long time, Davo had said they were a sign of rain. More recently, Dad had said it was a sign of carrion nearby. The giant bird continued circling. Maybe there was a dead roo or sheep carcass nearby. He couldn't smell the scent of death, but there was something else tainting the air. He cautiously peered over the edge of the cliff. The drop below made his head spin.

Clayton clasped onto the branch of a eucalypt to steady himself. Blowies ganged up on him, but he didn't have the energy to swat them away. He slumped against the tree trunk, deflated.

"You are not well," the Red King cackled. "Delirium from my heat I imagine."

Dust swept over the side of the plateau and merged. The Red King rose into the air, a tangible shape with face and arms. "It is time to go home. There is nothing more you can do."

Why would Waringa lie? Why would he tell him he could defeat the Red King? Clayton looked for the rifle. It lay on the far side of the plateau where he'd crawled out of the cave.

"I've had enough of you," said the Red King. He blew hot dry wind. It tore across the ground, lashing Clayton's t-shirt against his back. In the gusty wind, grasses struggled to maintain their foothold on the brittle ground. The rank grass flew across the dirt like mini blades, stinging Clayton's legs and ankles.

Hot air and dust blasted him, prodded his limbs, boiled his blood, and thumped his bones. The demon hurled dirt and stones against Clayton's bare burned legs. He tried to stagger towards the rifle, but the wind blew him back.

He grabbed the tree trunk as the Red King's breath unsteadied him. His gusty wind intensified. Sticks as large as limbs flew across the plateau. Some fell over the edge of the cliff and clattered against the rocks below. Clayton's hands, slick with sweat, began to slip on the tree trunk; his feet skidded against the dirt. He looked behind him at the edge of the cliff. Immediately, he shut his eyes and hugged the tree, trying not to dwell on the long drop below.

Against the roaring wind, there was the faint sound of metal grating against stone. He looked down. The rifle tumbled a few feet in the wind. If the Red King blew harder, Clayton thought he might be able to grab it.

Clayton laughed. "Is that all you've got?"

Chuckling resonated on the wind and another gust scorched him. The dust burned his eyes, but he kept them focused on the rifle tinkling along the rocks.

"Really? That's just lame."

"Why you weak, insolent little . . ." The Red King's cheeks extended like a puffer fish and he blew.

The rifle dislodged in the wind and rolled across the ground. Clayton dived and grabbed it in both hands before it fell over the edge.

Shielding his eyes from the dust, Clayton stood and braced himself against the tree trunk. His trembling hands fumbled with the rifle.

From the swirling dust, an arm extended in his direction. *Safety? Where's the safety?* Clayton's hands shook as he cocked the gun.

The demon's arm swung towards him, and Clayton took aim and fired.

The jolt of the blast felt like someone thumping him in the chest. The rifle ricocheted from his hands and he stumbled backwards. His feet caught loose stones. For a split second, he saw blue sky as the Red King's body dissipated in a cloud of dust. But then he was sliding down the sheer slope. Clayton clawed desperately at the rocky escarpment and crumbling earth, trying to slow his fall. Sand grains and tiny rocks dug under his fingernails and grazed his arms like sandpaper until something clasped his wrist. He glanced up and saw Waringa's large body leaning over the edge of the cliff. His shoulder jarred as Waringa took his weight. Clayton wrapped his fingers around the spirit's furry paws.

Clayton peered down, trying to focus on his feet and not the long drop below. A small rock jutted out from the side of the hill and he shuffled his feet along the crumbling cliff until he could rest his foot and take the weight off his arm and shoulder. It wasn't far to the top of the plateau. With Waringa's help, he could find footholds and make his way up.

"Pull me up," he gasped, but nothing happened "What are you waiting for?" Clayton met Waringa's amber eyes peering over the edge. "Pull me up!"

"That," began Waringa, "I cannot do."

"What?" Clayton glanced down at the sheer escarpment and instantly regretted it. Sharp rocks jutted out like blades ready to shred his skin if he fell to the tiny dots below that looked like pebbles but he knew to be tussocks of spikey spinifex.

"Don't leave me. Don't you dare leave me."

"But you are alone. He left you," said Waringa.

"Davo didn't leave me. He'd never deliberately leave me."

"He left you, Clayton. He was weak, as your dad would say."

Waringa's grip loosened.

"Please." Clayton's cheeks ached as he fought to hold back tears. "Don't go. I need you."

"No, you don't. You are the warrior."

Clayton's foot slipped on the rock. He looked down, trying to regain his foothold, and jimmied his big toe into a tiny nook. "Please. I can't do this alone."

"Yes. You can." Waringa's voice was so calm, so steady. "We all have to face reality, Clayton."

"No. Just pull me up."

"How can you pull your father up if you can't pull yourself up? You need to face reality before your dad can. Your mum can't save him. Only you. You are the warrior. Your dad is going to fall."

Clayton looked down, half expecting his dad to be climbing up after him. Instead, he saw blurred earth far, far below. Dizziness consumed him. He shut his eyes, attempting to stop his head spinning.

"I don't understand."

"Yes, you do. You just don't want to admit it."

"Waringa, please. I can't do this."

"Yes, you can. You are strong. Strong enough to find the magic. Strong enough to pull yourself up."

Waringa released his grip.

"No!" Clayton reached up and grabbed Waringa's paw with both hands. Tears were running freely now. It would be so easy to let go. There would be no drought, no anger, no loss.

"Why did he let go? Why did Davo let go?" Clayton asked Waringa. "Why is Dad letting go?" Clayton dug his fingers into the fox's paw.

Waringa didn't answer him. Instead, he pried Clayton's fingers off his paw one by one until he dangled by just an arm. Clayton swung his free arm wildly until he spotted a tree root sticking out of the cliff face. He reached for the root and grasped it just as Waringa's grip on his other hand loosened.

"Why won't you help me? I can't do this alone." He looked down at the drop below and shut his eyes. "I'm not strong enough."

Waringa didn't respond. All Clayton heard was the wind rushing over the plateau and corellas squawking in the distance.

He looked up at the exposed tree root, its tawny withered bark dug into his skin. Waringa had vanished.

For a moment, Clayton hung onto the branch, praying he'd reappear.

"Waringa?" he called out.

"Clayton," a voice echoed back on the breeze.

"Waringa?" Clayton found a crevice in the rock higher up and thrust his other foot into the crack. "Waringa. Come back." Clayton extended his arm; his fingertips clasped a ridge of quartz running down the slope. He heard his name again, this time louder and more pronounced.

"Waringa. Wait!" Clayton shuffled his hand up along the branch and pulled with all his remaining strength until he rested his torso on the top of the hill.

Clayton lay panting on the cliff top. Energy drained from his core and all remaining hope dissipated into the dusty air. The gravelly plateau and dirt dug into his chest, but he no longer had the energy to care.

"Clayton."

There was that voice again, closing in. And footsteps. Vibrations pounded through the earth, or maybe that was merely his chest thumping. The pelting of sand grains against his legs subsided, and as the wind eased, the flies started buzzing around his exposed ear. He buried his head further in his hands, but somehow the flies continued their bombardment, descending on his listless exterior.

"Clayton!"

Now that the voice was more discernible, he knew it wasn't Waringa coming to save him but his father coming to reprimand him. Clayton no longer had the strength to care.

"Clayton." The voice was quieter, and Dad shook his shoulder. "Holy shit, Clayton." His voice crackled with concern.

Maybe he'd slipped away. Clayton imagined his carcass burning in the heat, surrounded by flies. Dad may as well put him out of his misery. There was nothing left. He'd failed. Clayton lifted his head slightly off the ground. The dust had settled. The Red King and Waringa had fled. But there were no rain spirits here and no water, just heat and flame and sun and dust.

"What the heck happened? Are you okay, boy?" Dad squatted beside him.

Clayton sat up and peered into his father's wide eyes. He shook his head. No, he wasn't okay.

Dad clasped Clayton's face in his calloused hands. "You scared your mother half to death." The concern bled from his dad's voice. "Heck, Clay. What's got into you?"

"The demon –" Clayton began and realised his explanations would be futile. Where was Waringa? He promised everything would be okay.

"For Pete's sake. Grow up and come back to reality."

Clayton bit his lip. "Like you?" His body trembled with defiance.

Dad didn't react. His eyes still maintained their impassive glare. They stared at each other.

"Can you walk?" Dad finally asked.

Reluctantly, and with his dad's help, Clayton got to his feet. He felt as if someone had driven a prickle chain over his skin and set to work on his joints with an electric auger, but his legs took his weight.

"The ute ain't too far." Dad walked towards the side of the plateau. "We'll call your mum from the car."

Clayton's feet fused with the earth. "I can't go yet," he whispered, his voice dry and hoarse. Waringa had promised meeting the Red King head-on would release the rain spirits, but the silent skies above were a featureless blue canvas. "I can't go yet," he repeated. He'd come so far. And for what?

"Don't be daft." Dad came back. "Your legs are okay, aren't they?"

Clayton managed a tentative nod.

"Then you can bleeding well make your legs walk down the hill."

The earth refused to release its grip on Clayton, and he didn't want it to. He shook his head at his dad and mouthed, "No."

"Look, you ain't in trouble," Dad said in a calmer tone. "Everything'll be fine. I even got you a new Akubra to replace the one you lost." He gave a shallow laugh and continued casually, "After that we could go to the pub for a steak sanga."

"I'm not him!" Clayton yelled over his dad. "I'm not him and I never will be. I'm me. And I'm still here. He might have left us, but I'm still ... here." Clayton choked on the last word. He couldn't hold back the tears now. He didn't care if his dad thought he was weak. He didn't care, period. The fight had left him. He'd fought and failed. And above him, the mantle of clear blue sky watched on with detached indifference, showing no sign that the rain gods were free.

Dad still refused to look him in the eye. "We should go and let your mum know you are –"

"Don't you miss him, Dad?" Clayton blurted out. He felt his dad's gaze turn on him with as much burning heat as the sun.

"– and we should fix that boundary fence and gate –"

"Davo's fence. Davo's gate." Clayton struck like a King Brown. "It's not just a fence. It's Davo's fence. I miss him. I miss Davo."

He watched the venom make its way through his father's body, making him convulse with fury. He had said his name, Davo. The one word never to be uttered.

Clayton slumped to his knees on the dusty plateau; defenceless, he waited for Dad's wrath to descend on him. The heat pounded on the back of Clayton's neck. Below him, the dry earth scorched his knees. Dad remained silent, and it sent chills through him. Clayton stared at the parched ground, avoiding eye contact. Ants marched in regimented fashion, carrying sand grains, preparing for the deluge that would never arrive. They carried twigs double their body length and reinforced their mounds with such hope and optimism.

The organised procession of ants suddenly turned into a frenzy of black dots running back and forth. There was another flurry of ant activity as a drop of water fell, creating a tiny crater of wet dirt. Dust billowed up as another drop fell. And another. Clayton looked up. Rivulets of water ran down his father's cheeks. And then Dad's knees folded up on themselves and he collapsed to the ground.

"I'm sorry, Dad. I'm so sorry." Clayton wiped his eyes on the bottom of his t-shirt. "I found him. I couldn't lift him. I fled. I couldn't . . . I'm so sorry," Clayton sobbed.

"N . . . no." His dad's body shook, and every time he tried to say something his voice cracked. "God . . . no!"

Walter's arms wrapped around Clayton, and he nestled his head in his dad's chest.

"It ain't your fault. If it's anyone's fault, it's mine for pushing him so hard, for not seeing, for not hearing him." Dad's voice caught in his throat as if he struggled to admit that. He took a deep breath. "But it certainly wasn't your fault, Clayton."

In Dad's arms, Clayton felt like he was in a sauna, but on the top of his head, the relentless pitter-patter of water drops took the edge off the heat.

Dad's tears fell faster, and the drops became heavier. Clayton glanced past his sobbing father to the sky: the beautiful dark grey, grumbling sky. Water trickled down Clayton's shirt, and dirt transformed to mud. Dad didn't notice, and Clayton didn't care. The rain spirits were free.

CHAPTER 16

$\longrightarrow$

Something stiff dug into the side of Clayton's neck.

After two nights at the hospital for dehydration and burns, with drips and tubes and monitors beeping by his side, he was glad to be in his own bed. He'd been so exhausted that his stay in the hospital had been a blur; even now he just wanted to keep his eyes shut and sleep. He had no intention of waking. But there it was again, a sharp-edged object cutting into his skin.

He pried an eye open. A drooling tongue lolled within inches of his nose. It waggled and extended ever so slightly, desperate to reach his face.

"Rusty!" Clayton sat bolt upright, and his forehead collided with a plastic collar around Rusty's neck. Still burned and tender from his ordeal with the Red King, Clayton's forehead stung as the plastic collar scratched his skin. But he didn't care. He hugged her around the neck.

Rusty nuzzled Clayton and tried to lick his ears but the plastic collar got in the way again.

"Poor girl. You can't reach." He leaned forward and let her lick his nose.

"How's Dad?" Clayton asked.

Rusty pawed at the bed with bandaged feet and sat down.

"Well, don't answer me then." Clayton patted Rusty's back and then walked to the bedroom door. He hesitated. Would Dad still be angry he'd run away? He didn't remember Mum or Dad saying anything while he was in the hospital. Every time he'd woken up, he'd just seen them sitting by his bed talking, but their words hadn't registered.

He pushed the door ajar and listened for yelling, or crockery being hurled around the house, but all was silent, except for a faint pitter-patter on the galvanised roof. As he entered the hallway, he heard muffled gasping coming from the lounge room. The last time he'd heard gasping like that was when he found Davo. Clayton ran. At first he thought the lounge room was deserted, but then he saw his mum's hair draped over the back of the couch.

"It's okay," she whispered. "It's not your fault. It's no one's fault."

He thought she was talking to herself, until he heard the sobs. Clayton crept forward. Dad lay on the couch with his head in her lap and his legs curled up on the lounge suite.

His mum glanced up as he approached. A tear rolled down her cheek, but she smiled at Clayton and mouthed, "Thank you."

Trying not to disturb his dad, Clayton tiptoed into the kitchen. It looked like it hadn't been cleaned in days. Dishes cluttered the sink, paperwork littered the table, and plates grew colonies of green alien life forms. He was surprised the dishes hadn't grown legs yet and run away.

"Sorry," Mum whispered behind him.

Clayton shrugged. "About what?"

"The mess. I'll clean it up later."

"Later is good." Clayton pulled out a seat and sank into it. "Will Rusty be okay?"

"Yeah." She sat down next to Clayton at the table and glanced back in the direction of the lounge room. "We had to sell off some of his . . . of Davo's things, but we should be able to afford all the treatment she needs."

Clayton took a deep breath and asked the dreaded question. "Is Dad okay?"

"He's fine, now. Thank you." She smiled again. It had been so long since he'd seen her crow's feet deepen like that.

Clayton stood and wrapped his arms around her waist.

"I don't know how you got him to open up, but thank you." She sniffed back tears and hugged him so tightly he could barely breathe.

"I gotta go fix that gate."

Clayton looked up to see Dad wiping his cheeks with the back of his sleeve.

"You want to come with me?" he asked Clayton. "You certainly made a dog's breakfast of it."

Clayton's heart sank. Dad said it so casually, as if nothing had happened, as if he was perfectly fine again. And why did he want to fix the gate?

"Walt, it can wait," Mum said. "Clayton should rest. And it's still raining outside."

"He'll be right. I ain't gonna make him work much."

Clayton got up from the table. "I'll get my Akubra."

Dad handed him his fishing hat, which was sitting on the table. "Come on, then," he said.

Dad spoke little during the long drive to Davo's paddock. Gazing out the window, Clayton wondered whether the rain had made his father any happier.

"Are you okay being up here near Davo's house?" Dad asked when they finally arrived after the long silent drive.

Clayton nodded.

"You sure? I wasn't thinking –"

"I'm fine."

Clayton looked towards the house and pictured Rusty running around the veranda, and barbeques, and watching the paddocks at dusk with Davo.

"I'm fine," he repeated. He only hoped Dad felt the same way. The rain had stopped now they were back at Davo's place. Hopefully that wasn't a bad sign.

Dad looked at Clayton for a long time and then nodded. "Okay then." He picked up the post-hole auger from the back of the ute with one hand. It looked like a high-powered steel corkscrew and was as tall as Clayton. His dad tucked the auger under one arm and a new wooden creosote post under the other.

Clayton followed his dad, carrying a much smaller and lighter cardboard box from the hardware store.

"Did ya take to the gate with a jackhammer or something?" Dad asked, removing the old, cracked post.

Although Clayton sensed his dad was taking the mickey out of him, he felt uncomfortable confessing how he'd destroyed it. "Is it easy to fix?" he asked.

"Yeah, no probs. We'll re-dig the hole, put in a new post, new fixings, reattach the gate and Bob's your uncle."

And why are you fixing the gate? was the question Clayton really wanted to ask.

His thoughts were drowned out as Dad yanked on the ripcord and the auger's engine rumbled.

"Ya wanna stand back," he yelled.

Clayton put down the cardboard box and took a few steps backwards. His dad's biceps shook as he leaned on the auger. The device vibrated against the ground and soon sweat beaded on the back of Dad's neck. On the other side of the fence, sheep retreated from the noise and jostled for shelter under Davo's veranda.

The grumbling of the auger finished. Dad dropped the creosote post into the hole and packed the soil in around it.

"Here, hand me the gudgeon bracket and top saddle," Dad said, pointing to the cardboard box.

Clayton peered inside to find a collection of odds and sods. He shuffled through the box, hoping to use his powers of deduction to work out what on earth his dad wanted. Nuts, bolts, l-brackets: he knew all those. He grabbed a U-shaped hinge and a weird bracket with a metal cylinder that looked vaguely familiar. Under that, he saw bits of metal attached to little white discs. He remembered seeing them on a fence once, too. *Gudgeon, gudgeon. Wasn't that a fish?* . . . He peered at the bits of metal in turn. None of them looked anything like a fish. Trusting his initial instincts, he handed the fixings to his dad and wrinkled his nose in anticipation.

Dad chuckled.

"What?" Clayton asked, with a sinking feeling in his chest.

"Good guess." Dad's laughter continued, crackling like snags on a barbie. It was so loud even the sheep turned to see what the commotion was about. There was depth to his laugh, but how deep it went Clayton wasn't sure. He had a sneaking suspicion Dad was only mending the fence so he could round-up the stock, herd them back here, shut off Davo's paddock and pretend it still didn't exist.

Dad made quick work of attaching the new metal hinges to the post. He lifted the gate back onto the bottom hinge, shut it, and fastened the latch. "What ya reckon? Good as new?"

Clayton watched with his heart in his throat as his father redefined the boundaries.

Under the veranda, sheep bleated. Clayton knew no one else was going to translate for them.

"So are the sheep going to be able to go to Davo's whenever they want?" asked Clayton hopefully. "There's a bit of feed still."

Dad started collecting the old hinges from the ground and threw them in the cardboard box.

"Dad?"

"Yeah?"

"It wasn't Davo's fault. Rusty, his farm . . . you can't just pretend they don't exist, pretend that Davo didn't exist."

Dad leaned on the gate and sighed. "I know." He looked at Clayton, tears starting to well in his eyes. "Did I ever tell you the Hopper gene was tough?"

It wasn't just a trickling of tears: it was a flood sweeping over his cheeks. Watching his dad cry, Clayton couldn't help but do the same. His cheeks hurt as he attempted to hold back tears, but it was no use. He'd tried. He'd tried so hard to lift Davo. He'd tried to reach the rope.

Dad's eyes were red rimmed, probably like his own were. "The Hopper gene is tough. But you . . ." Dad sniffed. "I don't know where you get your toughness from. You're so much stronger than I am."

He unlatched the gate, swung it open and put his arm around Clayton. They stood there for a long time, watching the sheep nibble on grass around the homestead.

"Are you okay?" asked Clayton, wiping his cheeks.

"Nah. Not really." Dad hugged Clayton's shoulders tightly. "But I will be. We will be." He grabbed the auger and handed the drill to Clayton. "Come on, son."

Clayton followed his dad back to the dust covered ute. There was a spring in his dad's step that defied his old bones, and a light in his eyes Clayton hadn't seen in months.

"You wanna help me lift this up?" Dad asked.

Clayton grabbed the bottom end of the auger although it was so light he expected his dad had really taken all the weight. As he set it down, he noticed a couple of fishing rods tucked along the side.

"What ya reckon?" Dad smiled. "Should we go have a gander and see if there are any fish in the dam?"

"Fish?" asked Clayton. "Don't fish need water? What are we fishing for? Midges?"

Dad snorted with laughter and huddled into the driver's seat.

"You'll be surprised. It rained the whole time you were in hospital. Almost felt as if the constant grey clouds were one of those spirits you go on about in your books watching over you," Dad said.

Clayton smiled. "Really?"

Corellas sitting on the fence next to them flew off as the ute tore across the paddock.

There was actually water in the dam when they arrived. Small birds twittered noisily among the saltbush and bluebush bordering the dam. The rain started up again, but as Clayton watched Dad fumbling with the rods, it all seemed inconsequential.

Clayton followed his dad down the side of the bank and tied on the sinker.

Dad cast his line. It missed the pool of water and thudded against the dry soil. "The wind must've caught it. That was headed right for the water."

Clayton sat on the bank; and Dad, after finding the water with his third cast, followed suit.

The air cooled; the birds ceased twittering and fluttering about, and silence settled across the dam. Perhaps Dad, like him, was remembering the time they were fishing with Davo. It was the last time Clayton remembered his brother truly happy.

"Ouch." Walter's voice broke the silence.

"What's wrong?" asked Clayton.

"Something hit my neck." Walter looked back across the plains. "Big mozzie maybe."

"Maybe." Clayton looked behind his dad's back, plucked a tiny object from the ground and held it in his fist.

"Davo used to do a trick when we were fishing where he flexed his muscles and made mozzies explode when they tried to bite him," Dad said.

Clayton nestled next to his dad and listened to his recollections. And while Dad attempted to unsnag his hook from an old submerged boot, Clayton looked at the object in his hand. A gumnut? Confused, he glanced around the treeless paddock and for a second, just a second, he thought he saw a fox scamper across the farm and disappear on the horizon.

If the themes in this story have caused you any distress, please reach out and talk to someone.

Helpline services in Australia

Lifeline
13 11 14
www.lifeline.org.au
www.lifeline.org.au/crisis-chat/

Beyond Blue
1300 22 4636
www.beyondblue.org.au

Kids Helpline
1800 55 1800
www.kidshelpline.com.au

Suicide Call Back Service
1300 659 467
www.suicidecallbackservice.org.au/

MensLine Australia
1300 78 99 78
https://mensline.org.au/

Thank you for reading PETRICHOR.

We hope you enjoyed it.

If you would like to be kept informed of further releases by Melanie Rees, or other new books from Hague Publishing, why not subscribe to our newsletter at:

www.HaguePublishing.com/subscribe.php

And if you loved the book and have a moment to spare we would really appreciate a short review. Your help in spreading the word is gratefully received.

ABOUT THE AUTHOR

Melanie Rees has loved writing and reading speculative fiction for as long as she can remember, but started taking it seriously after a failed kidney transplant to help fill in the time and provide purpose while hooked up to dialysis machines. Since then, she has published over 100 stories and poems in several anthologies by Black Inc. and Simon & Schuster, as well as in renowned magazines including Cosmos, Apex, Nature - Futures, and Aurealis.

She works as an environmental scientist, where she has spent a lot of time working on outback properties, wetlands, forests, and along the coast. When not playing in the dirt or stuck up a tree, she writes.

Petrichor was inspired by her time working with farmers in northern South Australia during the millennial drought and witnessing the malaise and heartache in both the community and landscapes. She wanted to capture that and address serious issues farmers were facing, but at the same time inject some "magic" into the story.

You can find Melanie and links to her other work online on Twitter (https://twitter.com/FlexiRees), Facebook (https://www.facebook.com/Melanie-Rees-Author-229382980460551) and at www.flexirees.wordpress.com.

Offline she resides on the picturesque Fleurieu Peninsula on a bushland property, and lives in a strawbale house that she built with her husband.

Hague

Publishing

www.HaguePublishing.com

PO Box 451 Bassendean
Western Australia 6934